BloodRite: Dominique

Sara Scott

Sara Scott
Email: sara-scott@live.com

First Edition: July 2009
Revised Edition: September 2012
Second Revision: November 2012

Cover photo by: Sara Scott

ISBN: 1479322199
ISBN-13: 978-149322190

I would like to dedicate this book to those who are and will forever be in my life and to the people who have crossed my path, if only for a moment, inspiring the creativity needed to write this book. Also, to those who have recently come into my life — I know you will be fueling the creativity needed to write the next.
I am truly blessed.

Acknowledgments

I would like to thank everyone who ever believed in my writing ability. As this is my first published novel, I am incredibly nervous, but those of you who believed in me fueled my ability to get this done and share it with the masses. To all my readers. I hope you enjoy this story and the characters as much as I have!

Preface

ALONE.

That's how Dominique McCloud feels as she sits on her plush king sized bed in the dark next to her open bedroom window. Rain trickles down the gutters as the rumble of thunder grumbles throughout the damp night. Lightening crashes nearby, lighting up the sky with its fierce strength. Dominique doesn't flinch; in fact, she invites the distraction from her chaotic existence, finding peace and serenity in each rumble and crackle. She pulls her pillow closer to her chest, laying her head on top of it. Straight, long black brown hair slides down her pale flawless cheek while she stretches the sleeves of her thermal shirt over her hands, balling the fabric in her palms, and sinking into the comfort of her warm bed. Dominique squeezes her pillow tightly, pressing her face deeper into the pillow, crying silently to herself.

Why is it that hindsight is twenty-twenty? If she believed in herself more, she would have recognized the signs of her life spiraling out of control. The hard way, she has learned that at any point, at any time, in any instant one thing can happen that will potentially change the outcome of her life. She always believed that major life altering events could happen to someone else, but not to her - especially since she came from a small town. Big things don't happen in small towns, right? She didn't realize at the moment that *it* was happening. Nor did she realize how vast her life would change. But, now that she sits alone in her room, she remembers that one event, that one person, that one thing that happened that has forever changed the way she thinks and how she will eternally make decisions. Before she even had the chance to realize what was going on, these events consumed her, and once she did realize it, it was too late to do anything about it.

But the more she thinks about it, the more she tries to collect herself, she might not have the desire to change the way everything happened. She has always held onto the belief that things happen for a reason. Fate, Karma, or whatever form of divine intervention exists, would make things happen the way it was suppose to happen no matter what she tried to do to change it. She knows that if she stops thinking this way she might go insane replaying her life over and over in her mind, trying to figure out the exact moment she could have done differently to change the outcome. But how can one exact moment be pin-pointed in order to bring about the desired outcome? Who's to say that no matter what detail was changed the outcome would not have been the same because that was how it was *supposed* to be?

Cynical? Maybe. Who wouldn't be after going through the kind of hell that would drive a sane person mad? What if everything you had ever known as truth was pulled out from underneath you – including who you thought you were? What if the foundation that you once stood on is no longer as firm as it once was, in fact, parts of it start to feel like quick sand. It can happen to you, don't think it can't. Small town people are not immune, in fact, they might be more at risk than big city people because in their small communities of comfort, they are not expecting anything big to really happen to them, or to those they love. And those people, those creatures, out there know this and they like to prey on this weakness.

These creatures look just like you from afar, but take a closer look and you will start to see the differences. Try really taking a look at your neighbor or your co-worker and you'll start to understand. Look them in the eyes, if they will let you. Look for signs of odd colored irises and over active pupils. Don't just assume they're on drugs. You might be the drug that they crave. Watch for extra sharp canines, or maybe they are a little longer than normal, because there are creatures out there that parade around this planet as humans and act as if they are just like you. As their population grows, it is their goal to mainstream themselves into the rest of society, but only when they feel the safety of numbers are in their favor.

They are tired of hiding.

They are tired of being second class citizens.

They are tired of being ignored.

Chapter 1

September

AUTUMN IS ONE OF THE MOST BEAUTIFUL TIMES OF THE YEAR in Tulare County, California. Not that there is a totally ugly time in the foothills smack dab in the middle of the mountains and the valley, but the changing landscape does help build the ambiance. With the change of the leaves comes the annual Harvest Festival held at the base of Badger Hill. This small town and the surrounding communities look forward to this event every year. Like most small towns, there's not a whole hell of a lot to do. Sports, camping, school, cow tipping, drinking next to the river, sex, drugs, working, yep, that about sums up the events of this area. Well, cow tipping does not necessarily happen all that often, but the tourists that drive through here to get to the Sequoia National Park get a good laugh when they ask, "So, what's there to do around here?"

The summer months are the worst for things to do. School is out which means school sports are done for the summer, which means more spare time. Unless you take the drive to Visalia to watch a movie or go to the mall, you're pretty much SOL. So, when the leaves start changing and the air starts to cool off, people start to get nostalgic for the upcoming year. It's the time of year when regularity and comfort swing back into action, including community theatre.

Dominique, a twenty-five year old astonishingly attractive woman with long dark hair that brushes her firm waist, perfect porcelain skin and dark green eyes, sits in the empty theatre with her feet propped up on the seat in front of her. Her five-foot, eight-inch frame is dressed in her usual casual attire of blue Levi's and a tight baby doll t-shirt. Today she chose black, which accentuates her striking features, bringing out her naturally dark black eyelashes and proving more that she does not need to wear makeup; her natural beauty is enough.

The building was originally built in the 1930's as a single screen movie theatre. In fact, it smells the way an old theatre smells; old. Restorations have been made with major effort to keep it looking like the original theatre; it is, after all, a historical landmark. The original movie screen has been replaced with a screen that can be lifted up over the stage with the push of a button creating space for stage acting to take place. These days the theatre is mostly used for independent films and community plays.

An audition sign for *Seven Brides for Seven Brothers* stands on an easel stage left. The stage floor has recently been painted a red-brown in preparation for the upcoming production. A tarp, roller brushes, and other painting supplies have been placed in the orchestra pit for easy access for the touchups that are needed once the paint has completely absorbed into the old wooden stage. Paint fumes have somewhat dissipated, but are still present causing Dominique to have a slight headache after her already long day of not so successful auditions.

Dominique shifts her body in the red velvet covered seat trying to stop her butt from becoming permanently fused to the chair.

She rapidly taps her pencil on her worn out script littered with director's notes while intently looking over the cast list.

"What did that pencil ever do to you?"

Dominique, surprised to see anyone in the theatre this late in the evening, looks up towards the sweet voice that has broken her silence. Tracy, with her curly blond hair pulled back in a pony tail, revealing her long slender neck, and dressed in gray trouser pants with cuffs that show off her long muscular legs, and a silky off-white long sleeved blouse, walks to the end of the stage and sits down on the edge. Dominique casually looks at the attractive woman sitting in front of her, mesmerized by her dark brown eyes.

"Are you here to audition?" Dominique asks, trying to reserve her excitement.

"Are you the director?" Tracy asks with confidence.

"Yes, but I'm afraid I have too many brides and not enough brothers."

"Well, you could call it Seven Brides for Seven Brides. That would add an interesting twist to the plot."

Dominique, feeling caught for having been checking her out a moment ago, unsuccessfully tries to hold back the embarrassment heating up her cheeks, "I could do that, but I'm afraid the Senior Citizens Committee holding the fundraiser for this year's musical might not think that was so witty."

"I don't know. I know some of those ladies; it might just be the inspiration they need to keep the old ticker running another decade."

Dominique laughs, "That's awful!"

"I know, I apologize," Tracy pops off the stage and confidently walks over to Dominique. Dominique puts her feet on the floor, "I'm Tracy Sanders," Tracy extends her hand.

"Dominique McCloud," she accepts Tracy's gesture.

"Nice to meet you."

"Nice to meet you, too."

"So, on a more serious note. I heard about this production at work and thought I would offer my expertise, if you have a need for a sound or lighting person."

"That would be wonderful. I can always use the extra tech help. So where do you work?"

"I manage a bookstore downtown, but I also manage music gigs, like at fairs and stuff."

Dominique frowns a little, "Wait a second, I know you. Tracy's Wonderland. You own that store, don't you?"

"Yeah, that's mine," Tracy admits, humbly.

"You've turned that place around! It's actually a place I enjoy going to now. Before it was dank and uncomfortable, like being in a crypt," Dominique stops, "I'm sorry, that was a rather bleak analogy."

Tracy laughs, "No, it's ok. I felt the same way. My grandpa had a rather bleak take on life, so I would say your analogy is appropriate."

"It was your grandfather's bookstore? Ok, wow. So, hi, I'm Dominique and I'm a jerk," Dominique extends her hand to reintroduce herself.

"No worries," Tracy laughs.

"How about I buy you a cup of coffee to make up for the insult?"

"How about you let me buy you dinner?"

"Serious?"

"Absolutely, why not?"

Dominique looks at her watch, "Sure, why not? I just have to lock up then we can go."

* * *

McFlanagan's, a pub style restaurant, is dimly lit by small lamps on each table. Each person who walks in is greeted with the smell of grilling steaks and onions. The waiters hustle about in their black pants, white button-up shirts and green ties efficiently serving their customers while the bartender carries a conversation with some rich old men who are avoiding going home to their bitching wives. Dominique and Tracy are sitting in a cozy corner of the restaurant, sipping their drinks.

"I love this restaurant. My mom and I come here all the time," Dominique admits cheerfully.

"Really? It's one of my favorites as well. My grandpa and I used to come here on Sunday's for breakfast before opening the store."

"So, you've lived here all your life?" Dominique asks while wrapping her hands around her glass like a security blanket. She observes Tracy's confidence and her sudden realization that as nervous as she is, she feels comfortable. As if they were two old friends getting together after a period of time.

"Yeah, I went to Diamante High."

"Really? Me too. What year?"

"Graduated in ninety-six."

"So did I. I don't remember seeing you."

"I was on independent study. I only stepped foot on the campus long enough to hand in my work and take finals. I got my diploma in the mail; I didn't even go to graduation."

"Why independent study?"

"My parents like to travel. They felt I would learn more traveling the world."

"How awesome is that? You've been everywhere? France? Spain?" Dominique asks, enthralled in the topic.

"Oui, and si. Everywhere, even the not so extravagant countries."

"I've always wanted to go to Europe. Visit the Thames, see the Rose, see theatre in the place where it began," she replies passionately.

"Why haven't you gone?"

"I was going to study abroad in college, but then my mom got sick so I didn't go. Time just took off from there; haven't really had the time since."

"I'm sorry. Is she ok?" Tracy asks reluctantly, afraid of the worst.

"She's ok. She had cervical cancer. Chemo really took a toll on her body."

"Oh, god, really?"

"Yeah, but she's doing better now. She's regained most of her strength."

The waiter walks up with his tray held over his head. He swiftly brings it down to the table and pulls off the first plate.

"Sirloin, rare, for you."

He sets the plate down in front of Dominique, careful not to spill the blood puddle that is forming under the slab of meat.

"And scampi for you. Can I get you ladies anything else?" he asks as he sets the scampi in front of Tracy.

"I'm good, are you?" Tracy asks.

"No, looks great. Thank you."

"Enjoy," the waiter tucks his tray under his arm and heads back towards the kitchen.

Dominique starts to cut into the steak. Blood oozes across the plate. Tracy looks at the meat, a little concerned, but not repulsed.

"Is that done enough? I can have them take it back if it's not," Tracy starts to signal the waiter.

Dominique takes a bite, "No, it's perfect."

Tracy puts her hand down, "Are you sure, it's kinda…"

"Rare? I'm anemic. I've gotten used to having to eat red meat like this. I've had to since I was little."

"Oh, ok," Tracy picks up her fork and takes a bite of her baked potato, satisfied with her answer.

"If this grosses you out I can have them box it up and eat it later."

"Oh, no big deal to me," Tracy continues to eat her potato.

"You're uncomfortable. I'll have the waiter bring me a box," Dominique waves at the waiter.

Tracy takes her arm and gently places it back on the table, "Seriously, it's fine. I'm not bothered at all. Enjoy your meal."

"You sure?"

"Definitely."

"Ok," Dominique continues eating her steak.

The hostess walks past, guiding an older couple to their table. The white haired, prudish, old lady gawks at Dominique's steak and tugs at her decrepit husbands sleeve.

"Look at that, Walter. She's eating raw meat!" she whispers, loudly.

Dominique blushes as she wipes her mouth with her cloth napkin. Their waiter walks past, she motions for him, "Could you bring me a to-go box?"

"No problem," the waiter responds promptly, striving for a good tip.

Tracy scoots closer to Dominique and throws a glance at the old hag staring at the meat. She pulls the plate in front of her and cuts herself a piece of the bleeding beef. Sensuously, she takes a bite and savors it.

"Mmmmm, this is fantastic," Tracy states with an orgasmic tone, "a girl could get used to this."

"Ah!" the old lady gasps as she drags her husband into another dining room.

Tracy laughs and slides back to her side of the booth. Dominique smiles. She's not sure if she should be embarrassed or flattered.

"I'm sorry, I didn't mean to embarrass you," Tracy tries to contain her laughter. She takes her napkin and wipes her mouth.

"No, it's fine. I…" she stops herself.

"What?"

"Nothing."

"Are you mad?" she asks, worried that she has offended her.

"No, it's kinda nice," she lowers her voice.

The waiter comes over with her with two boxes and hands them to her.

"Can I get you two anything else?"

"Just the bill, thank you," Tracy answers.

The waiter pulls a receipt book out of his apron and places it on the table.

"I'll be your cashier when you're ready."

Tracy pulls out a credit card and hands it to the waiter, "I'm ready."

He takes the card and receipt book and walks away. Dominique puts her meal in the box and closes it.

"Aren't you going to eat?"

"I'm not hungry. I had a late lunch."

"You sure? I've ruined your dinner. What a first impression."

"I told you, no worries. Seriously, I'm not going to allow you to apologize any more tonight," she boxes up her meal.

Dominique smiles as she wonders what the hell she is feeling about the woman in front of her. The feelings can't be mutual, can they? Tracy just popped in to help with the play, that's all, right? The waiter brings Tracy her credit card and receipt. She takes the receipt and signs it.

"Ready?"

"Yeah."

Tracy stands up and steps to the side while Dominique scoots out of the booth. As they are walking to the front door, Dominique starts to feel overwhelmed with embarrassment. She allows her hair to fall off her shoulders, covering her face. Tracy pulls open the front door, the bell tied to the handle clanks against the glass alerting the restaurant of their departure. Dominique walks down the sidewalk with her head hanging down.

"Hey," Tracy takes hold of Dominique's elbow.

Dominique turns around and looks up at Tracy's chin, too afraid to make eye contact.

"Ah, hey. Thank you for dinner. I'll see you later, right?"

"So, what? I buy you dinner and you brush me off?" she smiles.

Dominique looks up at Tracy, "You need to go, right?"

"Um, well, not really. Stop that."

"Stop what?"

"Stop being so unconfident."

Dominique gives her a curious look.

"Seriously. I've seen you on stage. You always got the lead in the school play. I've seen you give speeches to huge crowds. I know there's a confident women down there somewhere," Tracy states as she gently pokes Dominique's shoulder.

"I'm..." she stops herself, gauging from the raised eyebrow on Tracy's face, she probably shouldn't apologize again. She looks up at the sky, "Must be the full moon. It always puts me in a funky mood."

"I'll buy that. I know the power the moon can have on a mood."

They start walking down the sidewalk. The air is cool and crisp on this September evening. Soon winter will rear its ugly little head and walks will become miserable.

"Oh, do you?"

"Oh, yes. I own a bookstore, remember? I have books on astrology, biology, genealogy, all of those 'ology' books, you know?"

Dominique laughs, relaxing as she does, "So, you're stalking me."

"Stalking you?"

"Well, you've seen me do all of these things, yet I've never seen you. Therefore, you must be stalking me."

Tracy snaps, exaggeratedly, "Shucks, you caught me."

"Busted."

"You wouldn't just believe that I'm a big fan?"

She laughs, "A fan of small town school plays?"

"Well, when someone makes the national news for winning a small town script writing contest in high school, I'd say you caught my eye."

"You read that?" she blushes.

"Yes and from that point on I became your biggest fan, or stalker, whichever."

"God, that was ages ago."

"Whatever came from that?"

"A stage producer bought the short from me and is having it turned into a full stage production."

"That's cool. Do you get royalties from it?"

"Only if it makes anything."

"Are you writing anything now?"

"Not really."

"Not really?"

"Well, kinda. Here and there."

"God, if I had your talent I would write all the time."

"It's not that easy. I have to be inspired. I can't just write."

"What inspires you?"

"My dreams, sometimes. I have these crazy vivid dreams. So I start with that then embellish them and, voila, a story. The problem is that not all my dreams are so interesting. Other things inspire me too, though."

"Like?"

"New situations, new people. I people watch a lot and make up stories about them."

"Like that lovely old couple in the restaurant. They could be an interesting story."

"Exactly."

The wind starts to pick up, whistling its way through the maple trees. Some leaves fall to the ground and tumble across the deserted sidewalk. Dominique shivers and wraps her arms around her body to warm up.

"I should walk you to your car. It's getting cold."

"Actually, I walked. I live on Fern and Montgomery; not too far."

"Not too far? That's on the other side of town." Tracy looks at her in disbelief.

"Ok, so it's a little bit of a walk, but I like it. It's the only exercise I get these days."

"Well, at least allow me to give you a ride home tonight. As you mentioned, it is a full moon. Who knows what crazies are out there wondering the streets."

"How do you know I'm not one of those crazies?"

"I'm the stalker, remember?"

Dominique laughs, brightening up her face.

"You have such a beautiful smile."

Dominique's smile turns into a blush as they continue walking down the street, back towards the auditorium. Excitement wells up in Dominique's chest, her heart beating fast. She's been on dates with other women, but has not felt this way before. No one has compared to this. The only place to really meet other lesbians, safely, is at the social group that meets twice a month, but you get a very interesting smorgasbord of people at these events. There was Gertrude, or Gerry, a very butch woman whose biggest accomplishment was the ability to remove beer caps with her teeth. Then there was Jan, a little more femme, but a freakish vegan. That didn't work for obvious reasons. The topper was Melissa, totally psychotic and the reason Dominique stopped going to the social group and decided being single for the rest of her life was a much better alternative. The gravel crunches beneath their feet as they walk in unison onto the unpaved parking lot. Dominique looks around the parking lot for a car – all she sees is a black motorcycle dressed with matching saddlebags.

"Um, is that yours?"

"Yeah. Well, I didn't say it would be a warm ride home, but I do think I have a long sleeved t-shirt in there you can wear," Tracy states as she opens up the saddlebag. She pulls out a helmet and the t-shirt, "Here you go."

Dominique takes the helmet and shirt and looks at them. Tracy takes the food containers and puts them in the saddlebags and pulls out another helmet.

"You ok?"

"Well, you see, I don't ride motorcycles much, like, never, and um, I'm just a little nervous. I did just meet you and all," she awkwardly, yet cutely, rocks forward from heel to toe with her free hand tucked deep into her pants pockets like a nervous child.

Tracy places her hand on her arm and looks her in the eyes, "I've been riding since I was little. You can trust me."

Melting at the feel of her warm touch on her cold arm, Dominique pulls the shirt over her head, taking in the smell of the leather from the saddlebags with an underlying seductive scent that she can only assume is Tracy, and puts on the helmet, "Ok, ready," she smiles.

Tracy smiles and laces the strap under Dominique's chin and snaps it on securely. She gets on the bike and starts it up. The rumble of the engine fills Dominique's stomach with butterflies. Tracy puts her helmet on and then motions Dominique over.

"Go ahead and get on," she says while steadying the bike.

Dominique lifts herself onto the bike and sinks down behind Tracy.

"Just sit back and relax. Let your body move with the bike. Oh, and you might want to hold on," Tracy reaches back and takes Dominique's arm and wraps it around her waist.

Dominique slides her other arm around Tracy's waist. Tracy gives the bike some gas and releases the clutch. They start to roll down the parking lot; Dominique holds on tighter. Her heart races with excitement while the chilly fall air brushes her face. She eases up her grip, relaxing as she grows more comfortable. She folds her hands across Tracy's abs, noticing how firm they are. She blushes at her revelation, glad that she cannot be seen blushing again. She puts her face closer to Tracy and inhales deeply; confirmation fills her as she recognizes the same intoxicating scent from the long sleeved t-shirt. She tucks the scent into her memory as they slow down and turn onto Montgomery.

"Which one is yours?"

"The fourth house on the left. The one with the Beetle in the driveway," she says pointing at the hand me down powder blue VW bug she inherited from her mom.

Tracy follows the directions and pulls into the driveway. The quaint cottage style house looks as if it's right out of a fairy tale. The white wood shutters are opened against the thick stucco walls that look like they were frosted with a giant spatula. Sconces light up the entry way, illuminating the rounded red door. She comes to a stop and shuts off the engine.

"So, how did you like it?"

Dominique releases her hands, "It was wonderful! I loved it."

Tracy helps her off the bike, "Good, I'm glad."

Dominique takes off the helmet and hands it to her, "So, um, would you like to come in and have that coffee I promised you?"

"Sure, sounds good to me," Tracy gets off the bike and takes off her helmet.

They walk up to the door and Dominique pulls her keys from her pocket; only three keys hang from the Wile E. Coyote key ring. She selects the silver key and unlocks the door.

"I don't think I have ever met someone who carries so few keys."

"I hate keys. Sometimes I wish everything was done by code pads or barcodes. You know, implant a microchip in my hand, swipe it across the pad and ta-da, I'm in," she opens the door and steps in the house, flipping on the hall light as she does. She sets her keys in a homemade ceramic dish that sits on the entry way table.

"Ah, the mark of the beast."

She shrugs her shoulders, "Well, I already have that."

Tracy raises her eyebrow, confused, "Do share."

"I'm sure you have one too."

Tracy follows her into the house, looking around at the warmly painted walls and arched entries. Paintings of all textures and sizes décor the walls giving the house a comfortable artsy feel. They walk into the kitchen; Dominique flips on the light.

"Now I'm more confused."

"Social security numbers. Or the more recent fear of the mark of the beast, the microchips they put in animals."

"True. I guess anything can be construed as such."

"Here, let me have those," Dominique takes the food containers from Tracy, "Have a seat," she points to the directors chairs that stand in front of the bar.

Tracy makes her way to the chair, "You're house is very nice."

"Oh, thank you," she puts the food in the fridge.

"It feels so cozy in here. I love all the paintings. Who did them?"

Dominique pulls a coffee bag out of a cupboard and places it on the counter, "My mom did most of them, but a few of them are mine."

"Well, I already thought you were pretty amazing, but now this. I don't know if my brain can handle it."

"Oh, shut up," she says, jokingly.

"Feisty."

Dominique grins as she pours coffee beans into the grinder, "Absolutely."

Chapter 2

October

TRACY HAS JUST FINISHED PUTTING THE FINAL HALLOWEEN touches on her Wonderland. The walls and windows have been canvassed with black butcher paper, darkening the entire store. Cotton spider webs linger in the corners of the store with giant black widows hanging down from them. Iridescent ghosts glide back and forth across the expanse of the store on motorized fishing line. A soundtrack playing creepy music sets the ambiance and tucked between books lie motion detectors that emit scary cackles from witches and banshee screams while unsuspecting shoppers peruse the shelves.

A trio of young boys walk into the section of the store set aside for all of the Halloween related merchandise. They pull aside the black and orange streamers and walk through the doorway that has been made to look like a tombstone. They look around at all the decorations and walk over to the display of a witch sitting on an old wooden rocker in front of a bubbling cauldron. They look into the cauldron at the purple steaming liquid and start to reach their hand into it when the witch grabs one of their hands. The unsuspecting boy screams and runs out of the room while the other two boys laugh.

"Good one, Tracy!" one of the boy's exclaims.

"Why, thank you," Tracy calmly responds, standing behind them.

The boy's jump and whirl around towards Tracy, dressed in plain clothes.

Tracy laughs, "Gotcha!"

The boy's laugh again then look back at the witch, "Who's that?"

"Amy. She's helping me through the holidays."

"Let's go get Michael. We can scare him too!"

"Yeah!"

They rush out of the room, "Bye, Tracy!"

"See you later!" Tracy laughs as she watches them rush out of the store.

"Good job, Amy."

"Thanks. Staying still is harder than I thought it would be."

"Oh, I know it. I had a hard time not smiling when people would come in, that's a dead giveaway."

"No kidding."

The bell on the front door rings with the arrival of a new customer. Tracy looks out the doorway towards the front, "Keep up the good work," she whispers.

Amy gets back into position as Tracy walks back up to the register. A tall guy in his mid to late twenties, wearing a white ribbed tank exposing his very defined arms, pulled tight against his hard abs, obviously he works on his physique, blue jeans and flip flops walks over to the register. He runs his hand through his ear length wavy light brown hair that flows into his sideburns as he sets an accordion folder down on the counter. Tracy walks up behind the register and looks at the folder then up at his eyes.

"Cool contacts," she observes as she takes a closer look at his yellow brown eyes, "they're wolf like."

He rubs his hand through his hair again, "Um, thanks. I like them. Good for Halloween and all."

"Absolutely. How can I help you?"

"I was looking for the owner, or a manager."

"I'm Tracy."

"Oh, cool. Well, I'm Seth and I work at the blood bank down the street. We're doing a promotion to try and get people in to donate blood. A pint for a pint. Heard of it?" he opens up his accordion folder and pulls out a poster.

Tracy takes the poster and looks at the colorful display advertising the blood banks promotion with Baskin Robins, "Good poster."

"I was wondering if I could put it up in your window and if you would let us put a stack of these by the register?" he asks as he pulls out a small stack of miniature versions of the large poster.

"Sure, no problem."

"Great," he sets a stack of flyers next to the register, "I can tape it up for you. Is it ok if I peel back some of the paper?"

"Oh, yeah, go ahead," she pulls out her tape dispenser and hands it to him, "Just be careful not to tear it. I've been working on this all day."

He takes the tape from her, "Looks great in here. Very creepy. You like Halloween?"

"I love it. It's my favorite holiday."

He smiles and states, "You know it's not really a holiday."

"Yeah, but it should be."

"I agree," he states as he gently peels back the paper Tracy just stuck to the window, "Why do you like it so much?"

"I just really like the idea of celebrating harvest time and celebrating the other world. It's neat to think that for one night the boundary between the dead and the living is dissolved and the non-living get to walk the earth."

"Interesting. You have a sort of eclectic view of Halloween – Celtic and pagan."

"Yeah, I suppose I do," Tracy starts organizing the counter area.

"It's even more interesting that you use the term non-living instead of dead. Are we a believer of the immortal?" he asks, teasingly.

Tracy smiles shyly, "Well, I guess I like the idea. I'm sure vampires and werewolves don't exist, but I like the legends."

Seth laughs a little as he finishes putting the paper back over the window, "I didn't mean to embarrass you. I like to believe in that type of thing, too. It's always interested me," he sets the tape dispenser back on the counter and picks up his folder.

Tracy laughs, "Hence the eyes, I suppose?"

"Exactly," he turns to leave the store, but stops and turns back around, "You wouldn't be interested in a costume party, would you?"

"A costume party?"

"Yeah. There's a party at the DeFleur castle in a few weeks, you should come," he opens up the folder and pulls out an envelope sealed with crimson wax and hands it to her.

"Cool envelope!" she opens it up and reads over the card, "I've always wanted to see the inside of the castle. It's so mysterious."

"Yeah, that's the way the owners like it," he smiles at her showing his perfect teeth, "It's invitation only, so don't forget to bring the card with you if you decide to come. You can bring a date, if you like."

"Oh, well is it ok that you gave this to me?"

"Oh, yeah. The DeFleur's, they own the blood bank, gave all of us employees five invitations each so we can invite anyone we like. Since you like Halloween so much, I figured you would be the perfect guest."

"Awesome! Thank you so much. I would love to go."

"Cool. Don't forget to dress up. And be prepared to be impressed. It is an impressive party. Unforgettable."

"Thanks again."

"Thank you for letting me put up the poster," Seth heads out the front door.

"Oh, yeah, no problem," Tracy waves at him as he leaves. She examines the hand calligraphy invitation then puts it in her backpack, "Yay!" she says to herself as the excitement of the invitation wells up inside.

Chapter 3

BACK AT THE THEATRE THINGS ARE STARTING TO COME together. Some of the cast members are helping with the technical side of the production while others filter through gobs of old costumes to find the best ones for their country characters. Jordan, Dominique's best friend since senior year of High School, and Dominique are sitting on the floor of the stage looking over set designs. Tracy is up on the catwalk moving and testing lights with the other light techs. Dominique is having a hard time staying focused on the task at hand. She hasn't been sleeping well lately. Funky, depressing dreams. Some of them are actually horrific. At least she has a few story ideas.

"So, I was thinking vibrant yet simple," Jordan points at the design for the 1850's Oregonian town scene.

Focusing, focusing, "Ok, 'splain."

"Well, I've been to plays where they use the most minimal amount of props and sets possible and, frankly, they bore me visually. I like to see as much as possible to help set the tone, you know what I mean?"

"Sure, but we have to keep in mind transition time. If we take five minutes every time we need to change scenes we will lose the audience."

"Yeah, which is why I was thinking canvas backdrops that can be lowered in for the main visual, while props such as tables and chairs, etcetera, can be mounted to wheeled platforms with locking wheels. We have the budget to do this and the space backstage. Some of the rolling sets can be used in multiple scenes without notice by adding simple touches, like a table cloth to the table," she points to the paper.

"Alright, sounds like we're getting somewhere. How much time will all of this take? Can we get everything painted and set up in time to have more than adequate dress rehearsals?"

"That depends."

"On?"

"Whether or not you and your mom will help us with painting the giant pieces of canvas" she smiles sweetly, batting her eyelashes, an effective technique she has used on Dominique before.

"Ah, I see," she smiles at Jordan and pulls the scrunchy off her wrist so she can put her hair into a pony tail, "Of course I will. And I'm sure mom wouldn't mind as long as we make it as simple as possible. Give me rough sketches of what you're visualizing and I can draw the scenes on the canvas. That way all she needs to do is follow what's there."

"Can you ask her then?"

"Sure, but why don't you ask her? She asks about you all the time, she would love to hear from you."

"Does she?"

"Of course. You know, you were unofficially, officially adopted."

"Yeah, I know," she smiles, "I'll call her."

"Good," Dominique knows Jordan feels loved and accepted by her and her mom. Since coming out she was rejected by her family. Her parents are good Christian folk. Yeah right.

Tracy climbs down from the catwalk and walks over to Jessica, one of the other stage hands. Dominique flips over a piece of paper and starts to sketch out a background, but Jordan keeps an eye on Tracy as she reaches across Jessica to pick up a pair of pliers on a nearby table, brushing up against her as she does.

"Oh, sorry about that," Tracy flirtatiously states.

"Oh, no problem," Jessica responds suggestively.

Tracy takes the pliers and heads back over to some lights and starts to loosen the c-clamps.

"I hope you plan on taking it slow with her, Nickie," Jordan comments, worried for her best friend and long ago lover.

She puts her pencil down and looks over at Tracy, "Of course, but what's with the tone?"

"I don't know. There's something about her that just rubs me wrong. Sometimes I really like her, other times I'm not sure if she can be trusted."

"What do you mean?"

"Like the way she just accidentally rubbed up against Jessica to grab the pliers. She's such a flirt."

"Yeah, she is rather flirty, but I don't think she even realizes she is doing it."

"Doesn't it bother you?"

"I never really thought about it, until now. Besides, it's not like we are together. You know? We're just dating."

"Yeah, but with lesbians dating doesn't really exist. I just don't want to see a U-Haul in your front yard two weeks from now."

She gently pushes Jordan on the shoulder, "As if I would do that. We've already made it past the two week thing. We've been dating for a couple of months. And I've dated other girls and there wasn't a U-Haul involved. You and I dated, and we didn't move in together."

"Yeah, but we did talk about it."

"Yeah, we did, but we were friends for quite a while before we started dating," *Hmmm, where is this coming from?* "Are you ok? Am I sensing some jealousy?"

"No, of course not. We agreed that we make better friends. Besides, that was, what? Five years ago? We were twenty-one and dated for a month. I'm not jealous, just worried about my friend. Is that such a bad thing?"

"No," she leans against Jordan and puts her head on her shoulder, "I think it's great."

Jordan lays her cheek on her head, "Good, 'cause I'm not going to stop."

Though, maybe I do wish we never broke up. I really miss her, Jordan thinks to herself.

Dominique sits back up and looks at Jordan, "What did you say?"

"Good, 'cause I'm not going to stop."

"No, after that."

Jordan gives her a funny look, "Nothing...you ok?"

She looks at her watch, trying to ignore what she thinks she heard, "I think I'm hearing things. What do you say to wrapping it up and going out to eat?"

"Sounds good to me. What do you have in mind?"

"Crap."

"Oh, yeah, that sounds great," she teases.

"You know what I mean. Everything not good for us. Mozzarella sticks, buffalo chicken strips with lots of ranch dressing, hamburgers, milk shakes. Crap."

"I knew what you meant; I was just giving you a hard time."

"Cool, let's do it," she pops off the floor, "Ok, everybody, that's all for today. Thank you for all of your help, but let's get out of here."

Everyone starts to clean up their areas while the girls pick up their piles of paper and stuff them into Jordan's backpack.

Tracy walks over to them with her packed tool box and sets it down on the stage, "Hey."

"Hello," Dominique walks up to Tracy and hugs her, "Thanks for your help. Making any headway?"

"Yeah. Some of the clamps are rusted, but they don't look totally desolate. We should be able to get them to work."

"Fabulous."

"So, do you have dinner plans?"

"Yeah, Jordan and I were going to go eat, you want to come?"

"No, that's ok. I have to go do some inventory at the store, but maybe we could watch a movie later. Your house?"

"Sounds good. You bring the movie, I'll supply the popcorn."

"Cool," she picks up her tool box, "I'll see you later then. Nine ok?"

"That works."

Tracy kisses her on the cheek, "See you later, Jordan."

"Yeah, see you."

Dominique can't help but watch Tracy walk out of the theatre, "She is just so damn good looking."

"I won't argue with you there. Those carpenter pants define her ass well," she comments leaning her head to the side to look at her butt from a different angle.

She smacks Jordan on the shoulder, "You checking out my girlfriend?"

"Girlfriend? I thought you two were just dating," she mocks.

"Yeah, yeah. Let's go, turd."

Jordan smirks, "Well, you better take this turd and let's go eat some crap, ok?" she replies with an Okie twang.

She rolls her eyes and starts walking out of the empty theatre. Jordan is an incredibly extraordinary woman. She's always there for Dominique, compassionate, strong, and unbelievably good looking. What more does one need in a friend? It seems like ages ago that they dated. It was Dominique's idea to break up and be friends. She was too afraid of losing her if they got too deep into a relationship and then broke up. She sometimes wonders where they would be if they stayed together. Their friendship continues to intensify – not in a negative way, and it seems to grow stronger with each interaction.

They've been through a lot together. Prom, coming out of the proverbial closet, going back in. Luckily, the going back in phase was short lived. That really hurts the psyche. Jordan's parents were just so oppressive; Dominique feels truly lucky to have a mom who's happy that she's happy. She couldn't imagine the constant persecution.

Chapter 4

DOMINIQUE WRAPS HER ARM ACROSS HER ACHING TUMMY. SHE really shouldn't have had that last buffalo strip. No more crap nights. Of course she says that now, but next month, around this time, she will crave crap again. She decides to go to the bedroom to put on her pajama pants and ribbed tank. She hopes the stretchy clothes will help her feel better. God, if she just gets her bra off she would feel a hundred times better. A man must have invented those things.

It's incredibly dark tonight. It's as if the moon and the stars were ripped out of the sky eliminating any night light, though it's not overcast. She flips on some lamps and they seem to only brighten the area directly surrounding them. She walks into the hall and flips the light on, but she swears she turned it on already. The hall light doesn't seem as bright either. The hair on the back of her neck starts to rise up, sending chills through her entire body. She rubs her arms and scans the room. Sometimes she really hates living alone. Like right now. Her heart is in her throat – she swears the boogeyman is going to jump out from around the corner and grab her.

Walk faster, walk faster. I'll be safer in my bedroom, she thinks, *Ok, I'm nuts, as if any room would be safe from the boogeyman. Ok, I'm even more nuts, as if the boogeyman exists.*

And this is the beginning of how she gets herself in trouble. Sometimes her imagination takes over her reality. Besides, it's not like she can't take care of herself. She's had intensive martial arts training since high school – she learned from the best sensei in the area.

Just change quick. Tracy will be here soon.

"Nickie?" Tracy's voice calls from the hallway, as she makes it to the bedroom.

She automatically goes into a defensive stance as she finishes putting on her tank as Tracy pushes open the door.

"Whoa there, Sparky. Sorry I scared you. I knocked, you must not have heard me."

Relax, relax, relax, "It's ok. You knocked?" the house isn't that big, she should have heard her.

"Yeah, a few times. I found this on the front porch," she hands her a box wrapped in brown paper and sealed with crimson red wax on both ends.

"Thanks," she takes it from her and looks for the sender's name, "That's weird."

"What?"

"There's no label, just my name written on the wrapper."

"Do you recognize the handwriting?"

"No, but it's beautiful," she rubs her thumb over the crimson red calligraphy that spells out her name.

"You gonna open it?"

"Yeah, yeah. Let's go into the living room."

"Ok."

As they leave the bedroom Dominique tries to bring her pulse back down to normal. The last thing she needs is an aneurysm at the ripe age of twenty-five.

"You want me to turn off some of these lights? It's rather bright in here."

She flips off the hall light as they enter the living room, which is beaming, "Yeah. This has just been an odd night. I turned the lights on earlier and they wouldn't shine bright enough. Now I'm sure I'm making the power company very happy."

"Weird. Maybe you should have your electrical checked out."

"Yeah, maybe."

Now back to the odd package. She sits down on her favorite corner of the couch and starts pulling the seal away from the package, careful not to rip the beautiful calligraphy. She gingerly folds the paper and puts it aside. Beneath the wrapping is a stunning hand carved wooden box.

"Wow, that's impressive," Tracy states as she sits down next to her.

"Yeah, it is. It seems familiar. Like I've seen it somewhere before."

"Have you?"

"I don't think so, but this crest looks familiar," she rubs her hand across the crest and over the demons carved around it, "It's old."

Inside there's a letter written on parchment; the same crest is embossed in the wax that sealed the package closed. Beneath the letter is something wrapped in dark crimson silk. She pops the seal open.

"'In time all will be understood. – S'. That's it?"

"Who's 'S'?"

"I have no idea."

"Ooh, mysterious. Open the fabric."

She picks up the item and pulls the ribbon off. The silk slides off revealing an heirloom locket.

"Wow, that's gorgeous."

"This has to be a mistake. This is someone's grandmothers, maybe even great, great grandmother's locket. I shouldn't have it."

"Well, there aren't many Dominique's on this block; I'm sure they meant to give it to you."

She opens the locket, "Holy crap! That's me!"

"That is you!"

"Yeah, but older and in some sort of dress that's at least a hundred years old. This has to be a joke. A really good Photoshop job."

"Yeah, or maybe that is your great, great grandmother."

"You know, I would buy that except that I've seen pictures of my family on my mom's side and I don't resemble any of them this much."

"What about your dad's side?"

"That's a whole other can of worms. I don't know who my dad is or much about him. My mom doesn't really like to talk about it."

"Haven't you seen your birth certificate?"

"No. Every time I ask for it she diverts the conversation to something else or says that she'll take care of whatever I needed it for."

Tracy picks up the wrapper and examines the seal, "Wait a second. This looks familiar," she jumps off the couch and walks over to the television where she set down her backpack. She opens it up and pulls out the invitation to the costume party and hands it to Dominique.

"The seal is identical," Dominique states as she compares the two wax seals. She pulls the card out of the envelope, "You were invited to a party at the DeFleur Castle?"

"Yeah, a guy came into the store to put up a flyer and he gave me one. He said it was by invitation only, but thought I would really enjoy it since I love Halloween."

"Yeah, it's invitation only! Very few people have seen inside the castle," she sets the card and wrapper aside and looks again at the picture in the locket, "Maybe my father is one of the DeFleur's. But why would my mom keep that from me?"

"God, who knows? She was young when she had you; maybe they had some kind of falling out?"

"Oh, I know they did. She doesn't really clarify what it was about. Maybe he didn't want to have a child so young?"

"Well, I'm sure it wasn't on the top of your mom's list of things to do before graduating high school either, not that she didn't want you, but he should have taken responsibility too."

"Yeah, I know. It just sucks to think that my father is out there and for twenty-five years he didn't want anything to do with me. And now I get this on my door step."

Tracy scoots closer to Dominique and puts her arm around her, "I'm sorry."

"It's not your fault."

"Yeah, but it still sucks."

Dominique rests her head on Tracy's shoulder as she twines the chain through her fingers.

"Do you know anything about him?"

"Sure, I know some things. A lot of good stuff. My mom told me stories about how they met, some of the dates they went on. She told me she always felt safe and comfortable with him, like she could tell him anything and he wouldn't judge her. And he was quite the romantic."

"Oh, really?"

"Yeah, he would always surprise her with little notes and flowers. I guess she just wants me to have a good image of him and not know about what broke them apart."

"That's a long time to keep something this big a secret."

"I know. I'm just going to have to confront her on it."

Chapter 5

THE NIGHT RAIN HAS TURNED INTO A FINE MIST AS DOMINIQUE runs barefoot down a dark torch lit and damp cobblestone alleyway. Her heart is racing faster than she can run as she tries not to slip on the slick rocks. The terror of being caught and killed by the angry mob fills her body as she tries to pick up her pace, but the faster she tries to move, the slower she seems to go.

Rioters scream behind her while dogs bark loudly, threatening to rip her to shreds if she slows down any more. Her wet hair slaps across her eyes as she tries to look back to see how much distance she has. Quickly, she moves her hair off her face and turns forward, trying once again, to pick up her pace. She can see the lights glowing closer as she makes her way down the alley.

"The witch turned up there!" one of the angry rioters yell as she rounds a corner in her white night gown that is so long she has to hold it up so she doesn't trip over it.

Her breathing speeds up and she tries to keep her tears at bay. The last thing she needs are tears to slow her down. She tries to focus on her breathing and her ultimate goal of not being caught by the crazy people chasing her.

Why are they chasing me? Where am I? Why are they calling me a witch? she thinks to herself.

She continues running, but sees that she made a wrong turn and is heading towards a dead end. She quickly looks around for a place to hide, but she can't find a trashcan or dumpster anywhere.

"Hurry! We've got to find her and kill her before she corrupts anyone else with her devil mind reading!"

A little mind reading and everyone thinks you're an evil witch. I can't help that I was blessed with this gift. Who in the hell knows I can read minds? I haven't told anyone. I wasn't even sure I really could do it, she thinks to herself.

She scrambles to the end of the alley and finds nowhere else to go. She's cornered and she is going to be killed. She leans against the wall and slides down, burring her head into her knees, no longer trying to keep her tears inside.

The mob gets closer to her, soon they will be right on top of her. She will be hung at first light. No trial, just hung.

Screams start to ripple down the alley and the mob starts to retreat. She lifts her head and looks towards the screams, but sees no one. She stands and backs herself into the corner of the alley, trying to hide in its darkness. The screams start to lessen, but she is too afraid to move to see what happened.

A tall, slender, eloquent man dressed in a fancy suit and cape walks down the alley towards her. She tries too press her body further into the wall, hoping it will just open up and pull her in.

"My lady," he greets once he is about two feet away from her, "Come with me and you shall be safe."

He puts his hand out for her to take. She nervously pulls on her locket with her left hand. Somehow she knows this man, but isn't quite sure how; she feels relief seeing him. She reaches out with her right hand and takes his. He pulls her close to his body, so tight that she cannot get loose, then flies off into the night sky.

* * *

Dominique jerks awake and sits straight up in bed. She pulls the covers up to her neck, hoping to feel some comfort after her nightmare. Her hand brushes the locket and she reaches behind her neck to unlatch it. Holding it in her hand, she opens it up and looks at the eerie resemblance then snaps it closed, setting it on the nightstand. Her clock radio reads three in the morning, the witching hour; another long night. She rolls her head to pop her neck, then rubs it.

That dream was too real to be just a dream. It was more like a memory. Everything has been odd lately. She feels like she can hear people's thoughts, like Jordan's in the theatre. Not to mention the intense feelings of insecurity in areas she usually feels secure about. This emotional rollercoaster crap needs to stop before she goes nuts, which will be soon at this rate.

Chapter 6

DOMINIQUE SITS BEHIND THE COUNTER AT HER MOM'S gallery entering receipts into the computer, an end of day routine that does not necessarily happen every day. Today was a good day. They sold five original pieces to a tourist who was passing through on their way back home from the mountains. Fifty thousand dollars in sales; very good day.

Dominique marks the paintings as 'sold' in the virtual inventory data base that she spent a summer developing in hopes of helping her mom be a little more organized. Jade is much more creatively oriented than business oriented and Dominique was blessed with a lot of both. She inputs the last receipt and puts them into the locked filing cabinet in the back office. She starts back towards the sales floor when her cell phone starts singing *'Do you believe in life after love?'* by Cher, her mom's favorite song. She picks up after the first rendition.

"Hi, Mom."

"Hi, sweetheart. I'm sorry I had to leave early today, but you know your grandmother and her hair appointment."

Dominique chuckles, "I know. What happened anyway?"

"Her driver had some emergency and was going to be late, and that is not acceptable in Mrs. McCloud's life, you know. But everything is fine now. I'll come down and close up."

"Just walking out the door right now."

"Ah, no sales today, huh?"

"On the contrary. Try fifty thousand dollars in sales."

"What? Are you serious?"

"Of course, I'm serious. Would I joke about something like that?"

"Well, I would hope not. What sold?"

"The dancers."

"They bought all of them?"

"Yep."

"Fantastic!" she throws her hands up in the air and does a little happy dance.

"I did contain my composure until after they left, but I jumped up and down in the back room once they were out the door."

"They didn't pay by check, did they?

"Come on, Mom. As if I would let them do that. They used a credit card."

"That's my girl."

"So, Tracy and I were going to go to dinner, but would you like to come so we can celebrate?"

"Tracy, huh? You two getting pretty serious?"

"We're getting there. I really like her," she punches the alarm code into the key pad then walks out the door, locking it behind her. She starts walking down the street towards her little bug.

"She seems like a really nice girl, but she's the first serious relationship you've had in a long time and I am your mother and…"

"I know, Mom, you want me to be careful."

"Is that so much to ask?"

"I suppose not, but considering who you are talking to, do you think I would be anything but?"

"You're right. But some of the stories you told me about those other girls can really make a mother start to worry."

"I told you I met them at that lesbian social group. I never went back after the psycho lady."

"Ah, crazy, pierced everywhere, with the half shaved head and dreads on the other. She was fun."

"The best part was when we would be talking and she would suddenly start screaming at the imaginary squirrel running across the lawn," she opens her car door and gets in, locking it before she starts the engine.

"That was definitely the best."

"Tracy is nothing like any of those girls. She's down to earth, appreciates art, has traveled the world, owns her own business, and she likes me. What more could a girl ask for?"

"I guess. I just need to get to know her better, I suppose."

"So, come to dinner with us. We're having Italian at that place on Main."

"Ok, what time?"

"In a half hour. I'm going to go home and change first, then I'll go on over."

"Alright, I'll meet you there."

* * *

The small family style restaurant is busy for a Tuesday night. It seems that everyone has had the same idea of not wanting to cook dinner tonight. The waiters are quickly waiting on their customers, refilling drinks and bread baskets, while the drink waiter efficiently refills wine glasses. The heavy smell of garlic fills the restaurant while the sounds of succulent food sautéing moves through the air.

Tracy and Dominique are sitting patiently at their table tearing off pieces of their bread and dipping it in balsamic vinegar and olive oil. Dominique takes a sip of her iced tea then adds another blue packet to it and mixes it up.

"You seem a little nervous," Tracy observes.

"I guess I am a little bit nervous. This is the first time we all have sat down and had dinner and it's important to me that you two like each other."

"Well, from the brief contact I've had with her, I would have to say I like her. She reminds me a lot of you and I really like you, so what's the worry?"

"I don't know, just stressing, I guess," she wipes her mouth with the cloth napkin and puts it back in her lap, "She's here."

Dominique slides her chair back and waves so that her mom can see her. Jade waves back then makes her way towards their table.

"Hi, honey. Sorry I'm late," she kisses Dominique's cheek.

"No problem. Everything ok?"

Jade sits down and puts her napkin in her lap, "I was having wardrobe issues. No big. How are you doing, Tracy?"

"I'm doing well; it's good to see you again."

"It's good to see you too. I was just telling Nickie that I wanted to see more of you."

"I've been meaning to come by the gallery to see your paintings. I'll have to make it sooner than later. Especially since I hear they are selling by the bundle, congratulations."

"Oh, thank you. Today was not a normal day in the sales department. Not that I'm complaining. Did you guys already order?" she starts to look around for the waiter.

"Yeah, I ordered for you, too. Chicken Parmigiana."

"Ah, you know me well. Thank you."

"Madam," the beverage waiter politely interrupts, "May I pour you a glass?" he holds a bottle of red over his arm that is draped with a towel.

"Oh, yes, please."

He pours her a glass and then makes his way towards other tables.

Jade smells the wine then takes a small sip. She shrugs indicating that the wine isn't too bad and sets the glass back on the table.

"Not the fifty-year old Bordeaux, huh Mom?"

"No, not quite, but not bad."

"Fifty-year old Bordeaux?"

"My dad was a big spender, apparently. Spoiled her on good wine and now she's been searching for a decent equivalent."

"Yeah, I officially consider myself a wine snob," she says, jokingly.

"Or connoisseur. Not necessarily snob," Dominique smiles at her mom. It's obviously an inside joke.

"I've always wanted to try different wines. We'll have to take a trip to Paso Robles or Napa and go wine tasting."

"Sounds like a fun trip. We can stay overnight and make a weekend of it," Jade responds.

Dominique takes a drink of her iced tea and relaxes in her seat, internally ecstatic that they are getting along. She doesn't know what she would do if her mom did not approve. Her mom is her rock, her constant. Having to choose between the two would be unbearable.

"So, how's rehearsal going?"

"Good. The sets are coming together, thanks to Tracy, and Jordan is the perfect assistant director."

"Oh, how is Jordan doing?"

"She's doing great. Still working at the high school as a counselor. She really likes it."

"Good, I'm glad she's enjoying it. Wasn't she going back to school for something?"

"Yeah, she decided to take a break. She's tired of school for now."

"Understandable."

"How long have you known Jordan?" Tracy asks as trying to show the slight jealousy that is starting to manifest knowing they have history together.

Jade looks at Dominique, not sure that she should field the answer to that question.

"Since high school. We actually dated for a short while."

"And you're still friends?"

"Yeah, odd, I know. It was one of those things where we realized we were better friends."

"Oh, ok," Tracy takes a drink.

"You ok?"

"Yeah, just odd to be friends with exes, don't you think?"

"I guess it could be, if the relationship lasted longer than a month, but we were friends before that and she really helped me through a rough patch."

"Ok, no big, just curious. I suppose I would be concerned if you dated longer."

Dominique raises an eyebrow, then decides to take a drink of tea and bring up the possible jealous monster later. She subconsciously starts fiddling with the locket around her neck.

"Where did that come from?" Jade asks, reaching over to touch the intricately designed white gold.

"Oh, yeah, I've been meaning to tell you all day. We were just too busy."

"Ok."

"It was on my front porch last night in this really incredibly carved wooden box. And, this is the most interesting part, look," she opens the locket and shows her mom the photo.

Jade's eyes widen as she takes in the spitting image of her daughter. She sits back and takes a long drink of her wine.

"Who is it from?"

"I'm not sure. The note was signed 'S' and it came packaged in brown paper and sealed with wax. The crest on the seal was exactly like the one on an invitation Tracy got to the DeFleurs' annual Halloween party. Know anyone by that initial?" Dominique asks, knowing that her mom knows who it could be from.

"Hmmm, not sure. I'd have to think about it."

Dominique looks at her mother, not believing the response, "Come on, Mom. Do you know who it's from?"

"I'm not sure, honey," which is sorta true. She can't be exact since both of the DeFleurs' she knows have names that start with the letter 'S'.

The waiter comes over and starts to put plates down in front of them. Dominique takes a closer look at her mom and suddenly feels a wall between them; not a feeling she usually gets from her. They usually share everything.

"Mom?"

"Honey, let's just eat before it gets cold, ok?"

Dominique drops the topic, getting her mom's uncomfortable hint about the subject. She always avoids talking about her dad's side of the family where, this obviously, must have come from. She'll have to divulge some day.

"Nickie tells me you plan special events, like the concert coming up for the Harvest Fest."

"Yeah, the bands are really coming together. I think we're gonna have a really good turnout. I checked the online ticket sales and half the arena is already sold out."

"Oh, that's really good. I don't remember the turn out being that good last year."

"That's because Tracy didn't head up last year's concert and they had boring bands there. Not to mention lack of advertisement," Dominique interjects.

Jade takes a bite of her Chicken Parmigiana and nods at Tracy, "I noticed that, too. There are a lot of really fabulous posters around town advertising the event. Did you make those?"

"Oh, no. The sponsor made those up. I gave my two cents, but they were in charge of it."

"Who's the sponsor?"

"The guys that put on the haunted house every year. They thought marketing the concert would better the entire event."

"Oh, I'm sure they're right. I've heard more about the carnival this year than I have in the past. And I know more people who are actually interested in going this year."

"Who puts on the haunted house, anyway?"

"It's run under a corporation. I've never actually met the guys face to face; only via phone and email. It's called New Blood, International. I guess it's owned by the DeFleurs' since the invite came from them."

Jade starts to take a drink of her wine, but chokes on it a little. She quickly sets the glass down and picks up her cloth napkin.

"You ok, Mom?" Dominique starts to get up to help her mom.

Jade motions her to sit back down, "Oh, I'm ok. Just went down the wrong pipe," she tries to recompose herself.

"That's an interesting business name. Guess it works for people who run a haunted house," Dominique points out.

"Are you sure you're ok, Ms. McCloud?"

Jade puts her napkin back on her lap and takes a drink of water, "Oh, yes, thank you. And don't call me Ms. McCloud, alright? Jade is fine," she reaches over and pats Tracy's hand.

"Ok," Tracy smiles at her, "The corporation actually owns a string of blood banks across the world, including the one in town. The proceeds for the haunted house actually go back into the company."

"Oh, that's really cool," Dominique states.

Yeah, that's really cool. Jade thinks to herself, *If people only know what was really behind the corporation, they might not think it was so cool.*

"You're not going to the party, are you, Nickie?"

"I planned on it. Why?"

"I don't know if it's such a good idea."

"Why? A costume party for Halloween sounds like a good idea to me."

"I've just heard bad things about their parties – drugs and such."

"Mom, I'm twenty-five years old and Tracy will be there. We'll be fine. I promise not to give in to peer pressure," she responds, not totally understanding her mom's conservativeness – she's usually much more encouraging of the things she wants to do.

"I just really don't want you to go."

"Why? Because of this?" her voice creeps up an octave as she holds up the necklace.

Jade sighs, knowing that it's not a topic that she is ready to have to explain, "Go if you want. Just be careful."

"Why won't you talk about it?"

Jade finishes chewing her bite of chicken, "This isn't the time or the place. We'll talk later."

Dominique rolls her eyes. If she had a dollar for every time her mother told her they would discuss the infamous topic later, she could have retired when she was sixteen. Maybe the DeFleurs' are her relatives. She could bypass her mom and go to them directly, but what would she say? *Hi, you don't know me, but I think we're related?*

"What will you go as?" Jade asks, trying to lighten up the discussion.

"Hmmm? What?" Dominique asks, pulling herself away from her thoughts.

"To the party. What will you go as?"

"I'm not sure yet. Maybe a vampire."

Jade sets her fork down and takes a long drink of wine, finishing the half empty glass in one big swallow. She flags down the waiter to pour her another as she sets the empty stemmed glass down.

"Thirsty?" Dominique asks, surprised at her mother's abnormal guzzling.

"Like you wouldn't believe," the waiter refills her glass and as the final drop hits, she picks it up and drinks some more.

* * *

Dominique walks her totally inebriated mom to her car, slightly successful, attempting to keep Jade from falling on her butt on the way. Jade likes her wine, but overtly self-medicating is not the norm for her. She guides Jade to the passenger side of the car and helps her in; Jade presses her hand against the door and holds it closed.

"Hey, I can drive myself," she slurs.

"No, Mom, you can't. Now, don't argue with me and get in the car," Dominique responds taking on the parental role.

Jade starts to argue, but sees the determination in Dominique's eyes. It's the same look she would give her if the roles were reversed, "Ok," she moves aside so that Dominique can open the door.

She guides Jade into the seat and belts her in, then turns to hand the keys to Tracy, "Here's my keys. Thank you for doing this."

"No problem," Tracy takes the keys from her.

Dominique closes the door, "I'm so sorry. She's never done this before."

"Oh, god, don't worry about it," she hugs her briefly, "I'll follow you."

"Yeah. Just wait in the car when we get there. I'll take her in and put her to bed."

"Sounds good."

Dominique walks over to the driver's side of her mom's new VW Beetle convertible. It's the car she bought to replace the old seventy-six that Dominique inherited. She starts up the car then puts on her seatbelt.

"Thank you for driving me," Jade states with her head glued to the head rest and eyes closed.

"No problem, Mom," Dominique puts the car in gear and heads out of the parking lot, checking her rearview mirror for Tracy before she turns into traffic.

Dominique contemplates whether or not to breach any kind of conversation with her mom in her current drunken state as she drives instinctively to the home she grew up in.

"I'm sorry, honey," Jade states as her temples start to throb.

"No, Mom, I'm sorry for bringing it up in front of Tracy. I know you already don't like to talk about him. I shouldn't have made it harder by bringing it up in front of her."

"It's ok. I've kept things from you for too long."

Dominique blinks hard then quickly glances over at Jade, "What did you say?"

"I have a lot to tell you and it's about time that I did," she continues, "I just held on to the hope that you wouldn't have to be a part of their terrifying family. Not that your father is terrifying," she quickly corrects, "but your uncle, on the other hand, not the kindest person on the planet. If you can even call him a person."

"Wow, Mom. I've never heard you say anything that blatantly negative about dad's family before."

"Well, I never wanted you to think anything bad about them, sweetheart," Nausea starts to overcome Jade as she braces herself against the passenger door.

Dominique looks over at her mom, "You need me to pull over?"

"No, I think I'll make it."

"Just one more block."

"Ok, ok," she breathes in deeply.

Dominique hurries the car down the quiet street and pulls into the driveway. Jade flings open the door and projectile vomits across the driveway and into the shrubs. Dominique quickly turns

44

the car off and rushes around to pull her mom's hair out of her face.

Jade puts her head between her knees and takes a few more breaths, "I feel better already."

Dominique holds her hand out for her mom to steady herself with and guides her into the house.

* * *

A half hour later, Dominique makes her way out of her mom's house and across the well-manicured lawn. She opens her passenger door and plops down into the old comfortable seat.

"I'm sorry that took so long. I had to help her wash her hair out. She got some vomit in it."

"No problem."

Dominique sinks into the passenger seat. Tracy pulls away from the curb and heads towards Dominique's house.

"Life has just been so crappy lately."

"What do you mean?" Tracy asks, trying not to take offense.

"Oh, I don't mean with you, honey. I've just had crazy nightmares that seem so real, this whole thing with my father, arguing with my mom, not to mention my anemia being out of control. You're one of the only good things going on right now."

Tracy smiles, "I'm glad I can be that person for you."

Dominique reaches over and takes Tracy's hand, "Me too."

As Dominique gets ready to settle in the comfort of Tracy's hand, her cell phone starts to vibrate, indicating a new text message. She reaches into her pocket and pulls out her phone. She slides open the face, revealing the keyboard and opens up the new message.

"Oh, it's Jordan. I sent her an email about the locket and told her I would call her later. Totally forgot," she starts texting her back with her apology and the promise to call her tomorrow.

"So, you guys are really close, aren't you?"

"Yeah," she responds as she slides the phone closed and sets it on her lap, "but it's not like you have to worry about anything."

"Oh, I didn't think so, I just…I'm not used to someone having an ex-girlfriend in their life. That's all. Just a little weird for me. My issue, not yours," she states, owning it.

"It's not like I'm friends with everyone I dated. Jordan is just, different. Like I said, we were friends before we were together. She helped me through a major part of my life."

"Coming out?"

"Well, that, and other things. But, I am too tired to talk about it all now."

"Yeah, long day," Tracy pulls the VW into Dominique's driveway and cuts the engine.

Dominique gets out of the car and meets Tracy at the driver's side. Tracy takes her hand and leads her up the walkway to the front door. She hands Dominique her car keys then holds both of her hands.

"I'm really glad you're in my life."

Dominique smiles widely, "I'm glad you're in my life, too," she pulls Tracy close to her and kisses her, "Thanks for going to dinner with me."

"Anytime," she hugs her tightly then pulls away, "See you tomorrow?"

"Yeah, I'll meet you at the fairgrounds?"

"Yeah. Just whenever you get up. No rush. I'm sure I'll have to debrief with Jim about how setup went tonight."

"Tomorrow's the start of your big concerts," Dominique states, proudly.

"Yeah, they'll be pretty good," Tracy states humbly, "but the last concert of the month will be the best."

"I'm sure they'll all be awesome."

Tracy smiles, "They all should have a decent turn out, at least."

Dominique unlocks her front door and opens it, "See you tomorrow."

"Goodnight," Tracy heads towards her motorcycle and pulls out her keys.

"Goodnight," Dominique walks into the house and stands at the door until Tracy drives away. She closes the door and locks the deadbolt.

She walks through the house, shutting off lamps that she left on for her late arrival and makes her way into the bedroom. She kicks off her shoes and plops down on her bed. One of these days she will actually let Tracy stay over. She longs to feel what it would be like to wake up next to her, all cuddly and safe. *Why does letting people in have to be so damn hard?*

Chapter 7

THE FAIR GROUNDS ARE ALREADY CROWDED WITH EAGER carnival patrons. As soon as the last bolt is fastened on the Ferris Wheel, the gates are opened. A young boy, around eight years old, wide eyed and excited drags his exhausted mother through the crowd towards the freefall ride, not caring who they bump into on the way. A nine year old girl stares open mouthed and amazed at her father who has just knocked down the heavy silver milk bottles with that tiny little baseball. A carnie pulls down a giant white teddy bear and hands it to the girl who animatedly accepts the prize. Her father eats up this moment knowing that in a few years, when she is a teenager, she won't think that he is so amazing. A group of teenagers stand off, away from the rest of the parental types, sneaking sips of vodka from their water bottles, thinking that the liquor can't be smelled on their breath by their unsuspecting parents, who are off drinking themselves. Dominique sits at a picnic table, staring off into the night sky while the group she's with continues with their conversation. Without a word, she stands up and starts walking away from the table, unnoticed. She pulls her lightweight sweater off from around her waist and slips it on as she walks along the grassy path towards her destination. Tracy, dressed in jeans that complement her nicely curved butt and a sweatshirt from her Alma Mater, is leaning on a fence that protects the crowd from the Ferris wheel, talking to a woman her age dressed all in black. Dominique walks up beside Tracy and wraps her arm around her waist, giving her a loving squeeze and kiss on the cheek. Tracy tenses up at the affectionate gesture.

"I'm not big on public displays of affection. I'm not the cuddly type," Tracy admits to the girl, avoiding Dominique all together. Dominique pulls her arms away and looks at Tracy inquisitively, but it's as if she does not exist.

"Yeah, I know what you mean. I hate PDA. It's like, don't cling to me – you don't own me."

"Ok, I get the hint."

Dominique, hurt, walks away from the girls. Tracy and the girl continue their conversation as they were before, not acknowledging Dominique at all.

Dominique forces her way through the crowd, pushing back tears of rejection, but the crowd seems to be growing, getting in the way of her escape. Keeping her head down, she tries to plow through the maze of people; she looks up momentarily to regain her sense of direction and sees a group of Goths walking towards her. One of the guys in the group stands out more than the others. His name is Sabin. She's not sure how she knows his name, but she recognizes him as someone from her past. Sabin glances at her with his deep, ice blue eyes, as if he is acknowledging her, but continues past her. Dominique stops and watches the group as they make their way towards Tracy and the other girl.

Beep! Beep! Beep!

The annoying scream of the alarm clock echoes through Dominique's bedroom, jerking her awake. She jumps up and smashes the alarm off. She runs her hands through her long dark hair, pulling it out of her face, then grabs the remote off of her nightstand and turns on the stereo. *Korn* spews out of the speakers as she rolls out of bed wearing a black ribbed tank and jammie pants. Dominique makes her way to the bathroom and turns on the shower. She opens up the cupboard and pulls a towel out and sets it on the counter next to her toothbrush holder that holds one lonely toothbrush.

* * *

The sun is shining bright on the cool fall morning at the carnival grounds of Dominique's dreams. The morning dew is starting to dry under the sun as the sounds and smells of the annual carnival permeate through the fairgrounds. The carnies are in full action, setting up their booths and double-checking the rides. The tech guys are taking sound and lighting equipment into the arena getting ready for tonight's concert.

"Everything should be smooth, Tracy. I talked to my guys last night about getting their shit together. They promised nothing like last night's run through would happen again," explained Jim.

"It better not. If one of those bands was up there when that platform gave way, we would have one hell of a lawsuit."

"I know, I know."

Dominique timidly walks over to them, "Hey."

Tracy's demeanor changes from frustrated to incredibly happy, "Hey, Nickie, just a sec," Tracy takes Dominique's hand and looks back at Jim, "Are we done then?"

"Yeah, don't worry about a thing. It'll be perfect."

"Alright, I'll be back at six to double check. I have my cell if you need to reach me."

"See you tonight. Nice to see you, Dominique."

"You too, Jim."

Jim walks into the arena and starts calling his crew together with his clip board in hand. The crew promptly stops what they are doing and congregate around Jim.

Tracy warmly pulls Dominique close and kisses her, "Good morning, sweetheart."

Dominique smiles, "Good morning."

They start walking away from the stage; Tracy wraps her arm around Dominique's waist.

"What was that about?"

"Oh, well, there was a little incident last night when they were setting up the stage. Seems that one of the workers came in drunk and didn't make sure one of the legs on the stage was locked. A crew guy was walking on the stage to make sure everything was level when the leg gave. He fell off the stage and broke his arm."

"Not so much fun."

"That's an understatement. So, after a breathalyzer test proving that he was drunk, I fired him. Not exactly my most favorite thing to do."

"Sure."

"But, on the bright side, tonight's concert is going to kick ass!"

"Who's playing?"

"Jesse's Band."

"You would think that a creative group of guys would come up with a better name for themselves," Dominique replies, preoccupied.

Tracy stops walking and faces Dominique. She takes both of her hands in hers and stares into her eyes, "What's up, Nickie?"

Dominique looks away, still overwhelmed by last night's nightmare.

"Come on, let's go sit by the river."

Tracy leads her beyond the fairgrounds down the trail to the river bed. Tracy sits down on a slab of granite and pulls Dominique down with her. They sit in front of each other with their legs crossed. Dominique picks up a twig beside her and starts to focus intently on it.

"The river's really full this year."

"Yes it is, but you're avoiding."

Dominique looks down at the twig she's breaking into a billion little pieces. A fidgety habit she does when she knows she's caught. Usually she can lead people to believe she's fine, she's a rather good actress when she needs to be.

"I just feel incredibly psychotic. I've never felt so insecure, scared, frustrated. God, I don't even know how to explain it. I don't want you to think that I'm a freak."

"I don't think you're a freak."

Dominique takes a deep breath in hopes of gaining courage. It doesn't work, but she asks anyways, "Does it bother you when I'm affectionate to you?"

"What do you mean?" Tracy takes Dominique's hands, causing her to drop the twig she was so intently focused on, "Sometimes I wish you were more affectionate."

Dominique looks up at her, sadness fills her eyes. Tracy scoots closer to her and wraps her legs around Dominique. She pulls Dominique close to her, embracing her.

"I wish I could take all of this sadness away."

Dominique relaxes her body in Tracy's warmth, "You do take the sadness away. You're the best thing that has ever happened to me."

"Did you have another nightmare?"

"They are so real, so intense. I try to think about other things before I go to sleep, but I keep on having these funky dreams."

"I'm sure it's your subconscious trying to help you remember your past."

Dominique pulls away gently, "That's too psychological this early in the morning."

"Seriously. There is so much of your life that you can't remember. Big things, like entire time periods."

"I know, you're right."

"Traumatic experiences cause involuntary suppression in order to protect you from what you're not ready to remember. Maybe your mind thinks you're ready for some of this."

Dominique looks endearingly at Tracy. She leans over and kisses her, "I love your brains."

They laugh.

Dominique looks across the river and sees a man in a long black trench coat standing with his back to them, she stops laughing. The man turns around and looks directly into her eyes, Dominique turns pale.

Hi.

She shakes her head of the very familiar voice that once again invaded her mind. He did not just get in her head, did he?

"What happened?"

Dominique gets up and pulls Tracy to her feet.

"Let's go."

Dominique drags Tracy away from the river and back towards the fair grounds.

"Whoa, slow down. What's up?"

"The guy standing across the river, he was in my dreams last night."

"Are you sure?" Tracy looks behind her, trying to get a look at him.

"Positive. I don't know how I know him, but I do. And I'm not getting a happy warm fuzzy feeling inside."

Chapter 8

May, 1977

IT'S 1977. A TIME WHERE PEOPLE HAVE JUST LIVED THROUGH make love not war, tie dye, tunics, tight bellbottom jeans, bare feet, and flower power. That's the way the majority of this generation lived, but there is a subculture of people who have fallen in love with the underworld. A world of vampire legends and werewolf stories. It's a world unlike their meager existence and a place where groups of people interact with one another and live in a fantasy world where they do not have to acknowledge a war in which they do not agree. Underground groups have started to gather in remote locations around the globe, more predominantly accepted in California, liberal capitol USA, where they can hang out and play out their fantasies. Some locations, such as Shadow and Sabin's castle that was built into the face of Badger Hill in the mid 1500's, is the perfect venue for such gatherings, or feeding parties, as they are sometimes called. It's exactly like a regular party with one minor exception…people allow themselves to be bitten and have others drink their blood. All in good fun and role play of the myth of vampirism, of course.

Shadow, a drop dead gorgeous man who looks to be in his mid twenty's, is lounging on a velvet covered couch holding a bong. The expansive vaulted ceiling living room is illuminated by rod iron candelabras and stuffed with furniture that accentuates the castle theme. Crushed velvet covered pods and couches make up the majority of the seating, all in black or crimson, of course, to keep up with the vampire façade.

People are sitting all over the room in groups of two and three. At first glance they appear to be enacting in a little ménage trios, nothing major. Take a closer look and you'll see a whole new definition to necking. Dominants straddle submissives, piercing the vein in their necks while another sucks the fluid from the wound. Not all of the groups are still feeding. Some are rejuvenating for the next round by feeding their souls with drugs while others are passed out on the pods.

Shadow closes his vivid green eyes and takes a hit from the bong then leans his broad, muscular body back into the couch, allowing the sweet smoke to fill his body. He rests his head back into the chair which shows off his manly chiseled jaw line and a hint of late afternoon stubble growing on his French-Italian chin. Appropriately, *Stairway to Heaven* engulfs the room, while other stoned partiers lie back, listening to the strings flow through the air. Shadow passes the bong to Jade, a very breathtakingly beautiful girl with an olive complexion, hazel eyes, and long black hair. She embraces the smooth glass that holds her mental salvation. Jade ignites the lighter and holds the flame over the stem. The bud crackles as the flame wraps itself around it. Jade inhales, coughing a little, then passes it to Moon. Jade scoots herself closer to Shadow and puts her head on his shoulder.

"Hey, Babe," Shadow embraces Jade in his muscle filled body. She nestles her head into his chest and tucks her hair behind her ear.

"I have to tell you something," Jade starts reluctantly.

"Ok, what is it?"

"You have to promise not to get mad."

Shadow looks down at Jade and kisses the top of her head, "You couldn't make me mad."

"I'm two months pregnant," Jade blurts out before she loses her nerve.

Shadow crosses his arms behind his head and takes in what he has just heard.

"Shadow?"

"Yes, Babe?"

"Did you hear what I said?"

"Yep."

"Are you mad?"

"I'm going to be a dad?"

"Yes, well, that is if you want to be a part of our life. I understand if you don't."

"You understand if I don't?" Shadow sits up and gently pushes Jade up, "What kind of man would I be if I were to abandon you now? I'm not going anywhere."

Jade relaxes and breathes a sigh of relief.

"When did you realize?"

"I just realized this week – it's my second missed period and now I'm having nausea."

"Let's go see Sabin. He'll tell us what it is."

Jade gives him a peculiar look, "Parlor tricks?"

"Something like that."

Shadow stands up, pulling Jade up with him. They walk into an adjoining room where Sabin, Shadows incredibly cocky fraternal twin brother, who is the image opposite of Shadow, not in stature, but in appearance and authority, is sitting on the couch with his arms around a girl on either side of him. Sabin glances over with his ice blue eyes at the couple walking towards him. He delicately pulls his long blond hair behind his ears then reaches for a mirror on the coffee table in front of him and snorts a line of the white powder.

"So, she told you?" Sabin directs the half question, half statement to Shadow.

With a flip of his hand he dismisses the girls sitting next to him, who comply instantly to this man who carries an air of authority.

Jade looks at Sabin, then at Shadow, confused. Sabin motions for Jade to sit next to him.

"Wait a second. What do you mean I told him? How do you know what I had to tell him?"

"There's just a glow about you, that's all. Please, sit."

Jade reluctantly sits down next to him on the couch. Shadow takes a seat in front on her on the coffee table. Sabin takes Jades arm and pricks it with his sharp pinkie nail.

"What are you doing? I don't consent!" she blurts out in accordance to the house rules.

"It's ok," Shadow takes Jade's other hand to comfort her, "he's not going to need much. You'll like this."

Blood starts to run down towards her wrist, Sabin's pupils constrict with pleasure at the sight of the blood. He drips a few drops on the mirror then licks the blood off her wrist.

"No use in wasting good blood," Sabin chuckles at his own witticism.

Jade looks at him with fear and frustration.

"Don't worry, darling, I'm not going to kill you," he states flippantly.

Sabin takes his pinkie nail and stirs the blood together with what's left of the white substance. The chemicals start to foam together changing from red to blue to pink.

"Look at that. It'll be a girl," he sits up straight and proudly clamps his hands together.

"We'll name her Dominique," states Shadow.

Jade looks at Shadow, "Stir my blood up in a little dust and you know it's a girl? Right," she rolls her eyes.

"It's accurate," Shadow assures.

"If it is a girl, why Dominique? Don't I have a say in this?"

"That will be her name. It is her birthright," Sabin responds as if it was not for her to question his authority, "That's the name of the slain Queen, our mother. She was an elegant and brilliant woman who ruled for a hundred years," Sabin takes a drink from a goblet of blood red wine from the table and stands up, "Your child will be born a princess, an heiress to the throne, and when you wed young Shadow, you too shall be a princess," Sabin walks around the table to his brother and hugs him from behind, "Congratulations, brother, you've found your queen," he tenderly kisses his brother on the cheek.

"But, I'm not ready to be married! I'm only sixteen!"

"You were ready to have sex with Shadow, that was rather adult of you," Sabin laughs a shallow laugh.

"I don't even know his real name. I'm not done with school," Jade pauses, taking in the rest of what she has learned. She rubs her forehead in an attempt to alleviate the haze. Did she hear him right? "What do you mean 'a hundred years'? You're not a king. You've had too much dust! I'm outta here!" Jade jumps off the couch and heads towards the front door.

The party suddenly becomes quiet; all eyes are on the spectacle. Jade approaches the front door, but as she reaches out to open it Sabin appears out of nowhere and blocks it. Jade jumps back, gasping in terror at the speed in which Sabin can move. She becomes disoriented and dizzy.

"I think we smoked some bad weed. Am I moving in slow motion?" The words start to trail off as she starts to pass out.

Sabin grabs her arm to steady her, "Soon you'll understand all you need to know," Sabin pulls Jade close to him. Their hearts start to beat loud and in unison. Sabin pulls Jades hair away from her neck then opens his mouth to reveal his growing incisors. Jade's eyes widen with fear.

"I did not consent to this, Sabin!" Shadow exclaims, instantly going to protect Jade. He gently pushes his brother aside, "Thank you, brother, for trying to take care of my problem, but I'm old enough to take responsibility for my own actions."

Sabin backs off, "Very well, little brother, I'll let you be," Sabin addresses the rest of the party, "Carry on."

The party starts back in motion. Shadow take's Jade's arm and guides her out of the house, into the night.

Chapter 9

THE FESTIVITIES ARE STARTING TO PICK UP AT THE fairground where there once was silence on this over cast afternoon. The Ferris Wheel carries a few young children whose parents would rather have them exposed to the kinds of people found at this event in the afternoon instead of the more rebellious crowd at night. Probably a good decision on their part. Joyful squeals echo from the free fall ride as the caged willing victims are dropped at outrageous speeds towards the ground. Sound checks are being performed in the arena while the rest of the fair prizes are being hung in their booths. Dominique and Tracy are sitting at a picnic table eating cinnamon rolls and drinking milk. They are watching Chris, the egotistical, athletic 'I'm the master at all sports' Martin, try to show off his super strength at the hammer. He motions for his *biffy tart (*a petite, frail, not so bright chick) girlfriend,

Amanda, to stand back. Chris heaves the ten-pound hammer over his head and thrusts it with all of his strength on to the metal plate below. The lights on the tall pole reach a quarter of its height followed by the whooping noise as it goes up and descends.

"It's ok, Chris, you can do it!" Amanda exclaims. Once a cheerleader, always a cheerleader.

Chris shakes off this minor defeat, "I just needed to warm up, it's comin'."

Chris picks up the hammer and heaves it up again. He slams it on to the metal plate. The lights rise up the pole halfway this time. Tracy and Dominique laugh at the sight of Chris' obvious frustration. What a dork. Chris throws them a dirty glance, then refocuses on his task. Tracy and Dominique get up from the table and throw away their trash. They walk over to get a closer look.

"Hey, Amanda, how are you doing?" asks Dominique.

"Oh, just fine. Living at home with my parents, going to school. Junior College is much harder than high school, though."

Dominique gives Tracy a funny look, "How long have you been going there now?"

Oh, let's see, about five years. But my counselor thinks I'll graduate this fall. How about you? Are you done with school yet?"

"Yeah, I graduated from the University last year," Dominique tries to make light of it, she's definitely the kind who would worry about someone else's feelings, "but there's no time frame for how long it should take to get through school. Everyone works at a different pace."

Chris shoots them a pissed off look, "I'm trying to concentrate here!"

"Oh, sorry," Dominique sarcastically apologizes.

Chris prepares for his final attempt. He winds back and smashes the metal plate, making a loud half growl, half yell as the hammer drops to its destination. Amanda and Chris watch the lights in anticipation. The lights crawl up the pole, slowing down the farther up they go. They reach a little over half way, stop, and then fall back down.

"There's something wrong with this damn thing! You need to get it checked out," Chris exclaims at the attendant while handing the hammer back.

Tracy hands the carnie four tickets and takes the hammer over to the plate, "Let me show you how this is done."

Tracy winks at Dominique.

"Yeah, like she's going to be able to do it," Chris doubts while sizing up the slender girl.

Tracy starts swinging the hammer on her left side, allowing it to gain momentum. She heaves the hammer over her head and slams it on the metal plate. The lights race up to the top of the pole, triumphantly hitting the bell. Small but powerful, what a woman.

"And we have a winner!" the carnie hands Tracy a Mighty Mouse doll.

"This thing is rigged!" exclaims Chris, ego smashed.

"No, sir, I can guarantee that this is not rigged. I run a clean operation here. I can't help it if the little lady is stronger than you are!"

Tracy, Dominique, and Amanda laugh. Chris' face starts to flush. He grabs Amanda by the arm.

"Let's go!"

He pulls Amanda away, "Damn lesbians!"

"Chris!" Amanda turns around and apologetically looks at Tracy and Dominique, "See you guys later."

Tracy and Dominique wave at her.

"Here you go, little lady," Tracy states using a southern drawl as she hands the stuffed toy to Dominique.

Dominique accepts the Mighty Mouse and curtsies, "Why thank you, my big, strong lesbian," Dominique slips her arm into Tracy's, squeezing her bicep.

They laugh at their sarcasm and walk away from the booth. Tracy wraps her arm around Dominique's waist, "So, what do you want to do now? We have three hours until the concert starts."

"I need to go home and change before the concert. It's supposed to really cool down tonight."

"Let's go back to your place then."

"Let's," Dominique agrees suggestively.

"What are you implying?" Tracy prods.

"I dunno. A little cuddling, a little kissing, a little…," Dominique looks around to make sure no one is in ear shot, "weed."

"You rebel!"

"I blame it on my parents."

Chapter 10

May, 1977

THE CRISP MAY AIR, THE LAST COOL BEFORE THE EVER PRESENT heat, presses itself against Jade and Shadow as they walk in silence on the dark cool country road. The eucalyptus trees sway their skeleton like branches in the intensifying midnight breeze. Jade has lost the buzz she had earlier; she wishes she still had it. At least that way she could somehow explain the shit that happened at the house in a semi-logical way. Wrap her head around it, well, pass it off as laced weed. Shadow escorts her off the road and onto a faint path, toward a fallen tree. He helps Jade sit down on the dead mass and then seats himself.

"Jade, I..."

"You're both real vampires, aren't you?" Jade interrupts.

"I've been meaning to tell you about this, but..."

"But what? But you forgot to mention it? You thought it was an insignificant detail? You thought it was better to let me believe that this was all a giant role playing game with a bunch of people infatuated with the myth? That vampires really exist and now I'm going to give birth to another one!"

"It's not that I forgot to tell you. Yes it is significant, but there was never a good time to tell you."

"I didn't know that vampires could reproduce. I thought at whatever age you are bitten that is the age you stay and you never grow old. Your human self dies. I thought vampires were a sexy legend."

Shadow lets out a sigh of defeat, "That's what we would like for everyone to believe. That way no one's after us like they used to be. Mobs of people would stake out our homes and burn them to the ground if they would merely suspect that we were living in the house. Innocent people were being accused and murdered because of it."

"Innocent people? What do you call your victims?"

"It's true, we were ruthless in our time, especially Sabin. He would find some hot young woman, or handsome young boy, and prey on them, saving some, killing others. Now we mostly go after fugitives, people in prison, or that should be. Or feeding parties with willing third parties and we only take enough blood to sustain life, we don't kill like before. We only kill if our position is being compromised, you understand what I mean?"

"So, if you think I'm going to tell someone about these parties I will be killed, right? You justify murder!" Jade jumps off the log and starts to walk back towards the path.

Shadow grabs her by the arm, "It's not murder! It's survival! You had a hamburger today, was that murder?"

"A cow is an animal! You're talking about human life! What gives you the right to be judge and jury to those who you believe should be in prison?"

Shadow lets go of her arm and relaxes his tone, "I can hear your heart beating right now. It's beating nervously, scared. But I can tell you are telling me the truth in what you say. My sense of hearing works the same way as a lie detector. Most of us can read minds." Shadow takes Jade's hand and places it over his heart, "Feel. Blood runs through my veins, my flesh is warm, I am alive in every sense of the meaning."

Jade starts to relax a little, comforted by the man in front of her. She's always felt comfortable with Shadow, more so than with anyone else in her life. He's the first person she has ever felt safe with…and he's a freakin' vampire.

"I respect you. I love you, which is why I'm going to give you the choice my mother did not have."

"What do you mean?"

"My mother was seduced by a vampire, a half breed like Sabin and I."

Jade gives him a peculiar look, "Half-breed?"

"My father's mother, my grandmother, was mortal. She was pregnant with my father when she was turned into one of us. Vampire blood flowed through her veins and into the veins of her fetus. We're different from those who are not born into it. My grandmother and my mother are true vampires, after they gave birth they could no longer reproduce, but we can. We were never bitten, per se. Our bodies have aged to the age of my father when he bit my mother and he is the age of his father. So, I'm giving you the choice. You can live forever, become one of us, or you can stay the way you are. Either way, your child, our child, will be born a princess and will one day be called upon to fulfill her duties."

"She will be immortal?"

"If you choose not to make the change, no, not until Sabin or I make her immortal. Her immortality comes from your mortality. We became immortal through our father changing our mother as soon as he found out she was pregnant; he didn't give her the choice."

"If I don't die she won't become a vampire?"

"No, she's a vampire in every sense of the meaning. She will have super human abilities that will develop as she grows. She will not understand her abilities or the limits of them until she drinks mine or Sabin's blood. Then she will understand who she is. Her sanity might become compromised if she refuses, making her rogue, and we can't have rogue vamps running around doing whatever they want to whomever they want. It's against the code."

"Oh, you have a code?" she responds, dryly.

"Of course. Similar to your laws, it's a way to keep our world less chaotic and a way to protect the human existence."

"Jesus."

"I'm pretty sure he had nothing to do with this."

Jade throws him a glance, then shakes her head, "So, help me understand this better, I'm giving birth to a child that will not be human! Fabulous."

"No, she will be half human, like me, but the full expanse of the situation will not start to be fulfilled until her twenty-sixth birthday or if she accepts the change prior."

"If I choose to stay the way I am, will you kill me once I've had her?"

"No, you will raise her and live what you would consider to be a normal life. Sabin is going to be furious, but I can subdue him as long as you don't try to do anything irrational. I'm sure he will still want you to marry me."

"I need to think about all of this," she looks over at Shadow and starts to grin, "This is all a joke, right? You and Sabin are two of the biggest pranksters around! I can't believe I fell for this! I must have smoked more than I thought." Jade starts to laugh hysterically.

"Jade, are you alright?"

Tears start to stream down her face as she tries to steady herself against the fallen tree. She grasps her waist, trying to control her laughter, "You aren't real vampires. There's no such thing as real vampires! We go out during the day, sunlight touches your skin. We've eaten Italian food together, and you know that it's pumped with garlic," she pulls a crucifix out from under her blouse and waves it in front of Shadow's face, "and what does this do to you?"

Shadow slithers away from Jade, "That's different."

"Whatever. Nice act," she inches the crucifix closer to him, "Let's not let the big bad cross hurt the poor innocent vampire," Jade takes the necklace off and starts swinging it in front of his face like a pendulum.

"I'm serious, put that away!" Shadow's voice turns into an animal like growl while his pupils dilate and his fangs become larger.

Suddenly scared by the man who used to calm her, she pulls the cross away from him and conceals it in her hand.

Shadow quickly explains, "The sunlight thing only applies to bitten vampires. When I was young Sabin used to tell me that the sunlight would kill me. Out of fear, I would hide in the shadows to stay away from the light that would peek into the house during the day. It was a joke he played on me for years, which is where the nickname Shadow came from. My real name is Andreas. The garlic thing is a myth. Who do you think started the myths about vampires? We had to do something to safeguard ourselves," he nervously chuckles, "not to mention humor ourselves. It was rather funny to see people walking around with garlic necklaces hanging around their necks. Everything smelt good for a while; we didn't have deodorant back then," he smiles at her.

Jade asks nervously, "But crosses aren't a myth?"

Shadow reaches into his pocket and pulls out a leather glove. He slips it on his well manicured hand and takes the crucifix from Jade. He lifts his leg up onto the stump, pulls up his pant leg, and presses the cross against his flesh. The cross becomes like an ember in a fire, sizzling his skin. Shadow winces at the self inflicted pain and removes the cross to reveal the brand.

"See, not a myth. Needless to say, we didn't start this one," he hands the cross back to Jade; Jade puts it back around her neck, "I love you, Jade. I would never do anything to hurt you. I will respect anything you choose."

Leaves start to fall off a nearby tree as the wind picks up in the darkness. A shiver descends down Jade's spine. Shadow stands in front of Jade and removes his trench coat, wrapping it around her shoulders. He fastens the top button, careful not to touch the unbearable cross.

"Well, isn't that quite the sight," Sabin applauds as he walks up to the couple, "an immortal falling in love with a mortal. You stupid boy!"

"Back off, Sabin!"

"I warned you about this. You should have taken her when you had the chance!"

"As if you've never fallen in love with a mortal! You've had the luxury yourself; don't blame me for your misfortunes!"

Shadow defensively stands in front of Jade, keeping a careful watch on Sabin's every move. Sabin jolts at the couple; Shadow quickly readies himself to defend.

Sabin laughs at him mockingly, "You think she won't turn on you the moment she has the chance?"

"She's not Isabella! She's different!"

"Mortals are mortals. You can't trust them."

"Shadow, I swear I will never say anything to anyone! Just let me be, let me make the decision!" Jade pleads.

"Oh, god. Shut up, woman!" Sabin covers his ears as if to shield himself from a painful noise, "Oh, please Shadow, please! Don't give me the gift of eternal life. Let me die of old age, let my flesh rot off my bones right before my eyes!" Sabin dramatically wraps his arms around his ribs, and thrusts his head back into the air laughing again, "I kill me! I really do."

Shadow shakes his head and endearingly places his hand on his brothers shoulder, "You never gave Isabella a chance. You just made her become one of us. And what happened, brother? Tell us, what happened to poor Isabella?"

Sabin brushes Shadow aside, "She was weak."

Shadow steps in front his brother, still holding on to his shoulders, "No, she was not weak. She was strong, vibrant, in love, full of life. You drained her of that life. She may have made the choice to spend eternity with you, but you forced her when she wasn't ready. You made her take her own life!"

"I didn't make her do anything. She was weak!" Sabin pushes Shadows hands off of his shoulders.

Shadow's voice becomes soothing, "Brother."

Sabin looks Shadow in the eyes. The pain of his loss starts to radiate as he lets his guard down.

"I've never betrayed your trust. Give me, no, give us the chance to try to mend the relationship between mortals and immortals."

Sabin straightens himself up, stripping himself of the vulnerability that was starting to shine through, "I'll give you this chance. If there is any sign of betrayal," Sabin turns and looks intently at Jade, "I will take her myself!"

And as fast as he appeared, Sabin was gone. Jade, eyes wide with disbelief, pulls the trench coat tighter around her body as to protect herself from anything that could harm her. Shadow guides her away from the fallen tree and back towards the main path.

Chapter 11

IT'S A DRY HOT MORNING, TYPICAL WEST COAST WEATHER. The scent of bleach and iodine engulfs the OBGYN waiting room. Jade, six months pregnant and already uncomfortable, sits next to Shadow flipping through the *Good Housekeeping* magazine. The baby kicks; Jade puts her hand on her belly and rubs it. Several other expectant mothers, some patient and others wishing they could induce labor, wait for their turn.

Betty, properly dressed in polyester slacks and matching blouse, walks in the waiting room with her purse appropriately hanging over her shoulder and her hair freshly done from the beauty parlor. She makes her way through the busy waiting room towards Jade. Shadow stands up to greet her.

"Hello," he kisses her cheek and guides her to sit down next to Jade.

"Hi, Mom."

"Gosh, this place is packed," Betty states while placing her purse beneath her seat. She leans over and kisses Jade on the cheek and rubs her belly, "How are you feeling?"

"Ready. She won't stop kicking today."

"That's how you were. Kick, kick, kick," she says in a baby voice to Jade's belly, "I bet she's as stubborn as you are as well."

"Thanks, Mom."

An overweight nurse pushes open the door with chart in hand, "Jade."

Shadow stands up and helps Jade to her feet. Betty takes her purse from beneath her chair and follows them out of the waiting room.

"How are you today?" the plump nurse asks.

"Oh, fine, I suppose."

The nurse directs her towards an open door. Jade makes her way towards the examination table and stands next to it. Betty and Shadow take a seat on the other side of the room.

"Well, you know the routine," the nurse states as she points towards the gown folded up on the end of the table, "The doctor will be in shortly," she shuts the door.

Jade pulls her shirt off and sets it aside. Her belly is the size of a basketball and as firm. She puts the gown on then slips off her pants and undies.

She motions to Shadow, "Help."

Shadow helps her struggle onto the table then stands next to the beautiful mother of his child.

"I picked up the cutest dress for her Christening at Macy's today. It's so beautiful," Betty states excitedly.

"Christening?" Shadow asks.

"Of course. She will be Christened in the church, will she not? I mean, it's one thing for you all not to get married in a church, but the baby must be Christened," Betty starts to get defensive.

"Of course she will be Christened, Mom," Jade states. Trying to calm the situation, she takes Shadow's hand, "It's important for me too. Of course I would want to be married in the church, but I have respect for Shadow's wishes as well."

71

"I just can't believe, Andreas, that you were not raised Christian."

"I guess it just was not important in my house growing up."

"It's not too late to accept Jesus Christ as your Lord and Savior."

"Mom, please."

Knock, knock.

Dr. Gillis, a woman of the feminist revolution, walks in the room with her stethoscope around her neck.

"How are we today?" asks Dr. Gillis.

"Ok," Jade responds.

Dr. Gillis walks over beside Jade and helps her lie back. She walks to the end of the bed and extends the stirrups. Jade puts her feet up in the cold metal and tries to relax.

"You would think after six months of this I would be able to relax."

"It's ok, sweetie. Some people have a hard time with this," Dr. Gillis responds, trying to comfort Jade, "Ready?"

"As ready as I'll ever be."

Dr. Gillis puts on her gloves and starts the exam, "So, do you have names picked out yet?"

"Dominique," Shadow responds.

"And if it's a boy?"

"It's not, it's a girl," Betty responds confidently, "She's carrying the same way I did when I was pregnant with her and the same as when my mother was pregnant with me."

"Sounds like proof enough for me," she removes the gloves from her hands and tosses them into the garbage. She takes the stethoscope and breaths on it, "Warm it up a little bit," she puts it on Jade's belly, "Well, everything sounds good. Good strong heartbeat and boy is she moving around."

"No kidding," Jades replies with a glint of happiness in her eyes.

"Well, Momma, see you in a month and take it easy."

"Thank you, Dr. Gillis," Jade responds as the doctor helps her back into a seated position.

"Take care of her, Dad."

"Yes, ma'am."

Dr. Gillis leaves the room. Shadow helps Jade with her clothes.

"How about lunch at McFlanagans?" Betty asks.

"Sounds great, Mom."

"Actually, I have to get going. Sabin and I are working on a business plan and almost have all the details worked out."

"That's fine. I'll get Jade all to myself."

"I'll see you later?" asks Jade.

"Of course," Shadow responds, kissing her on the cheek.

Shadow leaves the room as Jade finishes getting dressed. Betty helps her off the table then guides her out of the room.

* * *

Betty and Jade are seated in a booth at the restaurant looking at their menus and sipping their iced teas with lemon. Clouds start to form outside their window as a late summer storm starts to brew. Sprinkles start to spatter on the sidewalk and moisten the end of summer dryness that engulfs the town three months out of the year. Steam rises from the hoods of hot cars, the earth swallows the moisture, dehydrated from the summer scorch.

"You know, honey, you don't have to marry him," Betty states as she places her menu down in front of her.

"Mom, come on," Jade responds, still looking at her menu.

"There's something about him that I just can't put my finger on. Aside from the fact that he is not a Christian – nor does he plan on becoming one. He doesn't even come into the house when he comes over."

Jade sighs. She puts the menu down and takes a drink of her tea, "I haven't invited him in."

"Well, that tells me something about how you feel about him. You don't even want to invite him in."

"It's better that I don't."

"He's polite and well-mannered. Good looking and has the presence of a nice man, but...I don't know what it is."

"Mom. What do you want me to do? You told me that I had to marry him, that's the 'Christian' thing to do. You told me I could no longer live with you once I had the baby. You want me to move out on my own and raise this child myself? I still have to study for my GED and you want me to look into junior college. I can't do all of that on my own."

"I was upset when I heard the news, you know that. The shock of finding out that my child will not have the traditional path of marriage, then pregnancy just really hurts, you know?"

"I know that, Mom. It's not like I was trying to get pregnant."

"You can live with me as long as you need, if that means you will not marry him."

Jade looks out the window and stares off. The happy glint she had in her eye at the doctor's office turns into sadness. Betty reaches across the table and takes her daughters hand.

"What is it, sweetheart?"

"I don't want to marry him, Mom. I feel like I have to," tears start falling down her cheek.

"You don't have to do anything. I've already started turning the guest room into the baby's room this morning. I have the crib together and everything."

"I don't think I have a choice. He'll make me marry him."

"Well, I don't think so," Betty states defensively, "We can get a restraining order if we have to."

"Let me try talking to him. I'll do it tonight."

* * *

Jade drives her Beetle through the harsh rain up the hill to Shadow's castle style home. She pulls up to the expansive outer walls that are made of solid stone from the ground to the top of the tower. Not as large as a castle one might see in England, but it does extend a quarter of an acre and is as elegantly decorated as one might imagine a castle would be. A cobblestone walkway leads the way towards the thick massive wooden door lined with wrought iron and two dimly lit torch style fixtures.

Jade parks at the end of the walkway, takes several deep breaths and then pulls her umbrella out from the back seat before making her way towards the door. Rehearsing the conversation she will have with Shadow in her head, she lifts the ring attached to the mouth of the demon shaped door knocker and allows it to bang against the door. The door opens and there stands a servant dressed in a French maid uniform complete with a black velvet ribbon tied around her neck.

"Entrer," the maid states in French then moves aside so that Jade can pass through, "Shadow waits for you in the parlor," she states in her French accent.

Jade walks through the candle lit corridor towards the parlor. A fire illuminates the doorway signaling the room Shadow occupies. Jade takes another deep breath before entering then slowly steps in.

"Hi, babe," Shadow sets his book aside and gets up from his chair.

Jade walks over to him and gives him a hug, "Hey."

"How was lunch?"

"Well, actually, I wanted to talk to you about that."

"You don't want to get married," he states more than questions. He picks up his wine glass and gulps the last bit.

Jade looks at him quizzically.

"Sabin told me."

"Ah, right. The mind reading thing. How does he do that not being in the same vicinity?"

"He saw you as you were leaving the restaurant, but being in the same location is not always necessary."

"Fabulous. And he couldn't just let me tell you myself? What an asshole."

"He's only protecting me. Have a seat," he motions towards the plush leather couch. She sits, "Would you like some water? A soda?"

"No, I'm fine."

Shadow sits down next to her and leans against the arm, "Why don't you want to marry me?"

"I just. I don't want to be married."

Jade's heart starts to race.

Shadow puts his hand over her heart, "Don't lie. Tell me the truth."

Jade hesitates, then takes a deep breath, "I'm afraid of you. I'm afraid of Sabin. I don't want to bring my daughter up around him."

"He is her uncle. He would never do anything to hurt her," he calmly states with a defensive edge to his tone.

"But he would hurt me."

"In a heartbeat," Sabin quickly confirms, waling in on the conversation, "I told you, brother, you should have taken her when you had a chance. Now it's too risky for the baby. You'll have to wait until she delivers."

Jade tries to get up, inhibited by her belly, she is unable to get up as fast as she would have liked.

"She has not gone back on her promise. She has not spoken of us to a living soul."

"In time, Brother, in time. I think it best to kill her once she delivers."

"You're a fricken psycho!" Jade states, getting the rest of the way up.

Jade starts walking towards the door, "See, this is what I mean about not trusting him. Why should I?"

"Ah, ah, ah," Sabin holds her by the shoulders, stopping her from exiting the room, "It's best that you stay here until you give birth. In fact, you can give birth here."

"Let me go!"

"Let her go, Brother," Shadow walks over to them and removes Sabin's hands from Jade's shoulders, "Once again, I will not force her to do anything she does not want to do. She has proven to be worthy of my trust. I have more trust in this race than you do."

"Too much trust, if you ask me. She stays," Sabin takes her by the arm and pulls her down the hallway.

"No!" Shadow grabs hold of Sabin and pins him against the wall, "She can leave," he growls.

Jade pulls away from Sabin and hurriedly starts down the hallway, as fast as her pregnant body will allow. Intercepted by the maid, she is forced against Francesca's body with a knife to her throat.

"You stupid boy!" Sabin throws Shadow against the opposite wall, punching him in the face as he does so.

Blood trickles down his cheek. He wipes it off and as he does the wound heals itself. His pupils dilate and his canines protrude as he hisses at Sabin. Shadow leaps at him but Sabin knocks him onto the ground, jumping on top of him as he falls. Shadow swiftly gets out of the hold, overpowering Sabin. He pulls a knife out of his pocket and puts it to Sabin's throat.

"I will kill you, brother."

"You would kill me over a mortal?" Sabin asks, sputtering under the weight of Shadow.

"Yes, this mortal, I would. I love her. Something you'll never truly understand."

"You are right, I would not understand the betrayal of my brother for vermin!"

"That's just it! You look at mortals and see vermin. I see beautiful creatures worthy of life as much as we are."

"Get off of me!"

"First, promise you will never harm her."

"Fine, I will never harm her."

Shadow stares deeply into his eyes, "You nor anyone else!"

"I promise, not I nor anyone else shall harm your mortal," he responds, bored with his brothers incessant need for mortals.

Shadow gets off of his brother and helps him up. The maid walks back down the hallway holding a knife against Jade's neck.

"Release her!" Sabin orders.

The maid lets go of Jade and walks away.

"I will let you live under these conditions. First, you will never tell anyone of us."

"I already told you…"

"Silence!"

Jade does as she is told.

"Second, the child shall be named Dominique. Shadow's, name shall be on the birth certificate. Do you understand?"

"Yes."

"The child will be expected to live up to her obligations as our family. We will come for her when she turns twenty-six years old. If you try to conceal her from us, we will find you. Until then, leave my house," Sabin motions her away.

Shadow walks over to her and walks with her to the front door. He takes her umbrella that is sitting next to the door and hands it to her.

"I would like to see her once she is born, hold her, just once. Then I shall leave you be."

"I will have my mom call you on the way to the hospital."

Shadow opens the front door and lets her out. She hurries to her car and doesn't look back until she is in her locked car. She starts it up and puts it in gear, looking back one more time and sees Shadow closing the door as he goes back inside. She turns on her wipers and continues down the drive way. Why does she always choose the 'bad boy'? To spite her perfect high society mother? Partly. Ok, mostly. Truth is she's always been drawn to the 'bad boy' type since she was in pigtails and her mother caught her playing on the playground with the only black boy in school. It wasn't just that he was black, but his mother was their maid. It was ok for them to play in the privacy of their home, but not in public. No way would that have been acceptable.

What started as a way to show her mother that she could not control her has turned into chaos. Life and death. Mortal and immortal. But is there an inkling of love?

Chapter 12

Present

OCTOBER, A MODERN DAY MECCA FOR MOST VAMPIRES. A TIME and space for them to roam the earth as they are and not as they must pretend to be. For thirty-one days a year a vampire can sashay through the night without having humans stare at them or run away in fear at the sight of their fangs. For thirty-one days seducing an innocent victim is a much easier feat. People look at the October vampire as debonair, sweet, enamored by the great make-up job, "Those teeth look so real! How do you keep them on?" Most people are convinced that they are porcelain veneers. But, the point is, vampires have the opportunity to reminisce about the days when they could walk the earth without a care in the world. For some it's been hundreds of years, others only a few. Nonetheless, it feels like an eternity in hell for those that miss their normal routine, daily life, living and breathing, absorbing their daily allotment of Vitamin D from that golden ball in the sky.

Tonight, Saturday October eighth, is one of the nights that vampires here in Tulare County look forward to each year. Bonfires illuminate the sky while a mob of drunken teenagers and adults mosh through the fairgrounds rocking to the music of local bands. Sweaty, young, firm bodies with blood pumping forcefully through their veins celebrate this event while beautiful hungry vampires prey on their next unsuspecting victim by joining in the festivities. The haunted house, officially open this weekend, comes alive with lights and scary special effects awaiting the intermission from the bands. A few stragglers get in line and wait for the crypt keeper to open the door for their ten minutes of psychological torture.

Nineteen-year-old Jill Monty moves her petite frame towards the beer booth, shimmying on the over twenty-one wrist band she borrowed from Becky. She steps behind another customer, waiting her turn.

"Are you sure you're twenty-one?" a man's voice asks from behind her.

Jill jerks her head toward the deep sexy voice directed towards her. She peers up at the sexy blond man with the ice blue eyes and takes in a good look.

Nervously, "Uh, yes."

Sabin laughs, "It's ok. I'm not the beer police."

Jill smiles at him, "For that, I think you should buy me a beer."

Sabin steps back, places his open hand on his chest and bows his head, "Why, it would be my pleasure."

Sabin steps up to the counter and sets down fives, "Coronas."

The bartender pulls two bottles out of ice, pops the tops off and hands them to Sabin, "Here you go."

"Keep the change," Sabin hands a beer to Jill.

"Thank you," Jill takes a sip of her beer.

Sabin guides her away from the booth, towards the line that is starting to form at the haunted house.

"You know what I think?" Sabin asks.

"No, what do you think?" Jill responds, enamored by the sexy man in front of her.

"I think you should go with me into the haunted house."

"Oh, no. I hate those things. They scare the shit out of me. Besides, I don't even know you," she responds flirtatiously.

"Ah, come on. Sure you do. I'm the guy who bought you a beer."

"I should go. My friend, Becky, is waiting for me over there," Jill points towards her friend who is walking towards her with a man she does not recognize.

"Becky, who's this?"

"This is Shadow. He wants me to go in the haunted house with him."

Jill pulls her aside, snapping back to the fact that she's never seen these guys in her life, "Are you crazy? This guy wants me to go in the haunted house with him too, but I don't think it's the best idea. Do you?" she whispers as she steps closer to her friend.

"Why not? He's hot! Look at him."

Jill turns and looks Shadow up and down. His tight, black, thermal shirt accentuates his well defined muscles, "So he is, but seriously…"

"Stop being such a downer. Live a little. Your guy, what's his name?"

"Sabin, I think, but I don't remember him telling me that," she starts rubbing the frown that has formed on her confused head. Jill looks at her beer to gauge how much she has had, "I think this is going to my head."

"So, ladies, what did you decide? Are you going to go into the wittle scawee haunted house with my brother and I or not?" Shadow taunts a sarcastic baby tone, wiggling his fingers at them for emphasis.

"Your brother?" Jill replies.

"Yeah, this is Sabin, but you already knew that," Shadow teases, throwing a glance at his brother.

"I don't think so. Come on, Becky," Jill grabs Becky's arm and starts to pull her away.

"Ah, come on, Jill. Let's just go in. It could be fun," she pulls her arm away.

"I have a bad feeling about this. Something just doesn't seem right."

"We'll even pay for your admission," Sabin coerces.

"Free entertainment, come on," Becky pleads, pouting her bottom lip.

Jill sighs, "Fine. Let's get it over with," frustrated, she marches towards the back of the line.

Sabin walks over to Jill and extends his arm, "Come. Take my arm. We don't have to wait in line, I know the guy who runs this place. It'll be an experience you'll never forget."

Shadow smiles at Becky and offers her his arm; a shiver goes down her spine, but she takes it anyway. She immediately starts to relax on his arm; anxiety depleted. They walk to the front of the line, past grumbling patrons who snide at the couples bypassing the rest of the wait. Shadow nods at the crypt keeper who opens the door and lets the couples into the haunted fortress. Fog encompasses them as the door slams shut, closing pitch black darkness around them.

Silence.

"Becky, where are you!" Jill reaches her hands out in front of her in a panic.

"I'm right here," Becky puts her hands out, grabbing hold of Jill's arm.

"I hate these things! You know that! Don't let go of me," panics Jill.

"Ok, ok. I'll hold on to you."

"You two ready?" Sabin asks.

"I guess," Jill responds.

"Step forward," Sabin commands.

They do as they are told. Lightning flashes before them and banshees scream all around them. A sign illuminated by black light on the wall in front of them reads, "Don't move!" They freeze and cage walls fly up from the floor, boxing all four of them in. Becky and Jill scream, clinging tightly to one another as the cage floor below them starts to move down beneath the façade flooring.

Lights strobe around them as images of ghosts and ghouls fly around the abyss in which they descend. The boys laugh at the girls who are now fully embracing each other.

"Scared, ladies?" Shadow mocks.

The cage reaches its bottom and the barred walls slam open around them. The cavern is dimly lit by flickering lights dangling from the wood rafters. A musty dirt smell engulfs the room and water can be heard running through pipes. Sabin takes the lead, reaching out his hand to Jill, who willingly takes hold of it.

"I've never been in a haunted house this bad ass before!" Becky exclaims, still holding on to Jill's other hand, "Did you guys help build this?"

"Sort of," Shadow admits.

"How do they know when to send the next group down? Are there like cameras everywhere?"

"There are cameras in the main house, but you, my friends, are not going through the main exhibit. Only a lucky, select few are taken this way," Shadow explains.

"This doesn't seem too scary," Jill hesitantly admits looking around at the seemingly safe tunnel, "Does it get worse."

"Oh, just wait," Shadow chuckles.

They continue walking, silently. Jill releases Becky's hand and tightens her grip around Sabin's arm. Becky slides her arm into Shadow's. They reach the end of the tunnel where the path divides in two directions. Two coal mine style carts await their occupants, one in front of each path, both can only seat two people.

"What's this?" Becky asks, eagerly.

"This is the beginning of a wild and crazy ride. Are you ready for this?" Sabin asks.

"Yeah, let's go!" Jill declares, excitedly.

Becky looks at Jill with disbelief, "Guess you've changed your mind?"

"Guess so," she states, squeezing Sabin's arm.

Shadow lifts Becky into her cart while Sabin lifts Jill into his. They get in their carts and grab on to the levers.

"Ready?" Sabin asks Jill.

"Ready."

"See you on the other side, Brother."

Shadow nods while releasing the lever, putting the cart in motion. Sabin does the same.

The rickety bucket that holds Jill and Sabin creaks to a squeaky start as it heads down the tracks. It slowly picks up pace while the chilly air surges through Jill's long blond hair, pushing the tendrils over her face. She pulls her hair up in a pony tail, securing it with the scrunchy she has around her wrist. Her long slender neck glistens in the dimly lit tunnel. Sabin's eyes naturally gravitate towards her pink flesh. He puts his arm around her shoulders and caresses her skin with his fingers.

"You have amazing skin," Sabin whispers into her ear.

Jill nestles her body into his, "Thank you. This doesn't seem like such a scary ride. Where does it lead to?"

"The end," he tilts her head and starts kissing her neck.

Jill giggles, "I figured as much. We have to get out somewhere."

"Shhhh," Sabin breathes in her ear, "Relax."

He kisses her lips deeply, then makes his way back down to her neck. He nibbles a little.

"Hey, now. Don't leave a mark," she starts to pull away gently. She looks him in the eye, he smiles, revealing his growing canines. Her eyes widen in terror.

"What!"

Sabin pulls her close, she struggles to get away.

"Scary enough for you?" he growls as he sinks his teeth into her neck.

Jill's scream echo's down the tunnel as Sabin drinks her life away.

* * *

Becky clenches Shadow's arm in hope of finding safety from whatever caused the blood curdling scream echoing through the tunnel. Shadow holds her tight, pulling her head into his chest.

"Who was that?"

"A banshee, maybe a witch."

Becky releases her grip, "Sound effect?"

"Sure."

"Creepy."

"I thought you liked this sort of thing."

"I do, or did. I think my buzz is wearing off. How far to the end?"

Shadow puts his arm around her shoulder, "Just around the next bend."

The cart starts to slow down. The tunnel becomes brighter.

"Here we are."

Becky looks up ahead and sees the cart Jill was in, empty. Sabin is standing next to it holding a wine glass. She looks around the small entry in the rock wall surrounding a large wooden door adorned with wrought iron hardware.

"Where's Jill?" Becky asks as the cart comes to a stop.

"She had to run to the bathroom. Come in, join the party."

Sabin opens the door. Loud music intertwined with laughter and talking penetrates the tunnel, the sounds of a raging party. Shadow helps Becky out of the cart and leads her through the corridor.

"Will you show me where the bathroom is? I'm feeling kinda woozy," Becky holds on to her stomach as her face turns pale.

"No problem," he nods at Sabin who takes his leave, "this way."

Shadow guides her through the damp, cold castle. A fire is roaring in the stone fireplace, throwing shadows all the way to the top of the thirty foot ceilings. The rounded staircase is occupied by people dressed in black clothing, metal chains, and studs making their way up to the bedrooms. Couples are making out while others feed each other pills and mosh to the loud music.

"Water?" Shadow asks, grabbing a bottle from the platter the waitress is carrying and opens it for her.

"Yeah," she takes the bottle from him, "So, where's this bathroom?"

"Right here," Shadow opens the door, Becky steps in.

"Great, thanks," she takes a drink, "I'll be right out."

Shadow forces his way in and locks the door behind him, "Let me show you around. This isn't your average bathroom."

Becky, taken aback, "I think I can manage to use a toilet on my own."

Shadow swiftly walks over to Becky and gently slides the back of his hand down her cheek.

"Relax, beautiful. I won't do anything you're not willing to do."

Becky melts at his touch. The effects of the drug he slipped into her water surges through her veins. Shadow casually catches her and embraces her against his strong, well contoured chest. He gently swipes his thumb over her luscious lips then kisses her softly.

"Beautiful."

Shadow carries her over to the stone wall beside the built-in tiled whirlpool tub and slides over one of the rocks revealing a button panel. He types in the code and the walls separate. A stainless steel elevator opens up and he steps in with his catch, careful not to damage his goods. He pulls her body closer to his while pressing the button to the top floor, breathing in her sweet perfume as he does. His eyes constrict with pleasure. He caresses her neck with his lips; her pulse strong under his tongue. The elevator comes to a stop and he steps out into the expansive room that almost takes up the entire third story. The room is adorned with candelabras fixed to the medieval walls and sheer curtains dangle from the open windows and rafters. The full moon hangs brightly from the sky, illuminating the luxurious canopy bed set up in the center of the room. Shadow lies Becky down in the center of the bed and pulls off his shirt. His skin glistens in the moonlight, highlighting his well defined abdomen. He tosses his shirt aside and unbuttons her blouse, allowing it to fall open, revealing her firm soft skin. He kisses her stomach, tenderly making his way up to her breasts. He bites the center of the bra, springing it open. Her milky white, perfectly formed breast perk up at the touch of his caress. Shadow observes her breathing; gently up and down her chest pumps pushing her blood through her veins. He kisses her neck, then her lips. She starts to stir, moaning and trying to open her eyes, like when in a bad dream that you can't awaken from. Shadow pulls back and lies down beside her, watching her wake up. She blinks hard and looks around the room, confused. She looks down at her exposed breasts then over at Shadow.

"What? Where?" she asks, disoriented.

"Don't worry, you're fine," he responds, nonchalantly.

She sits up and takes her shirt to cover herself, "What did you do to me?" hysterically she picks up her bra and looks at the damage.

"Nothing."

Sabin walks in the room, clapping, "Way to go, brother. I gave her to you on a silver platter and you still did not take her."

"What does he mean, 'take her'?" she asks, scared.

Shadow rolls his eyes, "I want to give her the option. Something you've never believed in."

Sabin rolls his eyes, "Same story, new decade."

Jill, wearing a shear nightgown, walks in behind Sabin and puts her arm through his.

"It feels euphoric, Becky, you should do it," Jill walks over to the bed, opposite of Shadow and sits down next to her.

"What do you mean, 'it feels euphoric'? Being drugged and taken against your will? That is not my idea of a good time."

"Shhhh, calm down, sweetheart," Jill scoots in closer to her and takes her hand, "They are offering us eternal life. They need to repopulate the race. I feel so strong, so, so, alive! I can't explain it any better than that. It hurts a little, at first, like a pin prick, but then, it's wonderful!"

Though her mind still feels cloudy, Becky starts to calm down. She looks at Shadow and Sabin, catching Sabin's piercing stare. She looks him in his eyes and starts thinking that maybe it would not be so bad to have eternal life. To feel good and never be sick again. Have strength and the power to enamor anyone she pleases, even Jill, if she wanted. She looks over at Jill in her gown and slowly looks from her eyes to her breasts, so inviting.

She puts her hands on her head and rubs her temples,

"What are you wearing," she asks Jill.

"You like?" she asks, seductively.

Becky starts rubbing her temples, not completely comprehending Jill's response, "Where are these thoughts coming from?"

They are what you want. I am only regurgitating your desires. You have always been infatuated with Jill. Here is your chance, Sabin stares knowingly at Becky.

Becky looks back at him, "How did you do that? How did you get in my head?"

"It's a gift," he snaps his fingers causing the candelabras to light up. He snaps again and the room fills with music, "I'll leave you all to make your decision."

Sabin leaves the room. Shadow scoots closer to Becky and motions Jill to do the same.

"Immortal," Jill whispers in her ear, "A sense of belonging and forever taken care of," Jill leans in and kisses her cheek.

Becky turns her head to face Jill. She lifts her hand and touches her face. Jill leans down and gently kisses her lips. Shadow pulls Becky's shirt from her hand and sets it aside; Becky doesn't resist. Jill pulls off her gown while Shadow takes off Becky's pants, kissing her from stomach to thigh as he does. Jill presses her naked body against Becky's, lying beside her, teasing her nipples with her tongue. Becky moans. Jill slides her hand down Becky's stomach to her sex; Becky jerks at her touch and starts to sit up. Shadow leans down towards Becky's face, catching her lips with his, he kisses her deeply. He moves his mouth towards her neck and sinks his fangs into her pulsing vein, drinking her warm, young blood.

Chapter 13

TRACY IS LYING ON THE COUCH IN DOMINIQUE'S LIVING ROOM listening to the radio. The sun has set, allowing the blue hue of the night to penetrate the room. Tracy closes her eyes, relaxing for a moment before her big night at the fairgrounds. Dominique walks into the room, pulling a sweat shirt over her tight tank. Tracy takes in the beautiful woman before her, feeling pretty lucky to have her in her life. So modest or truly unknowing of how attractive she is. Dominique doesn't always have a low self-esteem, but it seems to come in waves, with the full moon or something, and tonight is a full moon. If she only knew how incredible she was. If she only understood where her insecurities came from.

"You could just wear the tank top," Tracy states, smiling suggestively.

"I could, but how would I fight all of those hot chicks off while you are on stage emceeing?"

"Good point. I don't want any trouble," Tracy states with her pretend tough girl attitude as she gets off the couch and approaches Dominique.

"I'd hate for you to have to jump off the stage and pummel some poor helpless victim drawn to my amazing beauty," Dominique exaggeratedly flips her hair over her shoulder.

"Me too," she wiggles her eyebrows then kisses Dominique, "Ready?"

"Yep."

Dominique grabs her keys off of the entry table and stuffs them in her pocket along with her ID and some cash. Tracy hands a leather jacket to her then puts on her own. Dominique stretches her neck from side to side then rubs her temples.

"You ok?"

"Yeah. I just had this weird pain all of a sudden. It's gone now."

"We can take your car instead, if you're not feeling good."

"Are you kidding? And miss an opportunity to press my body up against yours?"

Tracy shakes her head, "You're so bad."

Dominique smiles, "Why, thank you."

"Maybe someday we can try that naked."

"Ummm, of course, some day," Dominique's face flushes with embarrassment. Uncomfortable with the topic, she opens the front door and walks out, Tracy follows.

"I'm sorry. I didn't mean to embarrass you."

Dominique closes the door and locks it. She turns and faces Tracy, "I'm sorry for avoiding the situation. It's not that I don't want to, it's just that..."

"You don't have to explain. I'm a jerk for even bringing it up."

"No, you're not, I...I've never."

They walk over to the motorcycle and Tracy starts pulling out the gear.

"You're a virgin?" she hands Dominique a helmet.

"Well, not exactly. I've never exactly been with a girl."

"What about Jordan?"

"We never really went 'all the way'."

"Oh," she hesitates, "Have you been with a boy?"

"That's something I would rather explain at another time," she responds awkwardly.

"Oh, ok, I'm sorry, honey."

"No worries," she takes her hand, "I'm just not quite ready."

* * *

Fireworks fly through the night sky as the bands change sets. Tracy makes her way center stage and stands in front of the energetic crowd.

"How about that!"

The crowds cheers, loudly. Some lifting their beer bottles in the air, others flipping open their cell phone, a modern tribute to the old lighter flickering.

"Alright! Now, our last band of the evening," the crowd starts screaming in anticipation, "the one you all have been waiting for...Jesse's Band!"

Tracy steps off the stage as the drummer pounds his introduction, initiating the first song. Dominique meets Tracy at the bottom of the stairs and takes her by the hand.

"You want to get something to eat?" Dominique screams over the music.

"Yeah. We better before the booths close down."

Tracy takes her hand and leads them around the crowd towards the concession stands, trying to avoid the raging partiers.

"God, what a night!" Tracy states as they distance themselves from the madness, "I'm so exhausted. I just want to crawl into bed and go to sleep."

"I see nothing wrong with that. You've done a great job. It seems to be a success. How were the sales?"

"Oh, much better than expected for the first weekend," she replies, excitedly.

"Really? How much better?"

"Let's just say that I have a few plans that will make it to fruition," she replies, mysteriously.

Dominique puts her hand through Tracy's arm, "Oh, really? Like what?"

"Well, someone's birthday is coming up in a couple of months and I had a few ideas of what I would like to get her."

"And?"

"And, you'll just have to wait and see."

"Not even a little hint?"

Tracy looks to the side and puts her fingers on her chin, as if she is intently pondering the request, "Um, no."

"Fine. I'll work on my patience skills."

"Good. That'll be good for you," Tracy smiles and squeezes her tightly, "Now, what would you like to eat?"

Dominique looks at the menu above the booth, "I dunno."

"Well, let's see. We have junk food, French fries, which might be considered a vegetable, and more junk food."

"I'll go with a chili dog and a side of French fries. I wouldn't want to miss out on my vegetables for the day."

"Sounds good. Two chili dogs and two fries."

"Anything to drink?"

"Oooh, I could really go for a beer," Dominique responds.

"That does sound good."

"I'll go get us some. Meet you back here?"

"Yeah, I'll snag that table," Tracy points to a vacant picnic table.

"Cool."

Dominique walks towards the beer booth while dodging busy carnies making adjustments to their stations after the first run of the season. The Ferris Wheel's lights turn off so that patrons know they are closed for the night, but the workers still have a few hours of work ahead of them. The haunted house, the only ride not put on by the carnies, still has a long line in front of it. She makes her way up to the beer booth and pulls out some cash from her jean pocket.

"What can I get 'cha?"

"Two Coronas, with lemon, please."

"Alright," he pulls two Coronas out of ice and wipes them down.

"Guess the haunted house was a hit," Dominique observes.

"Oh, it's a hit every year. Haven't you gone in it?" he asks while popping off the beer caps and sticking lemons in the bottles.

"Oh, no. It's not exactly my thing."

"Ah, man. You're missing out on an experience. It's the best haunted house in the county. Hell, it's probably the best in the state. The guys who put it on really go all out. Everything looks so real," he sits the beers on the counter.

Dominique hands him some money, "I'm just not a big fan of being scared. I would like to see it in the daylight. I'm always looking for good set ideas."

He takes the money and hands her the change, "That would be the one to look at. Though, they would never let you do it. They are rather paranoid about someone taking their secrets," he hands her some change.

She sticks the change in a tip jar, "That's too bad," she picks up the beers, "Have a good night."

"You too."

Dominique heads back towards the table. She glances at the entrance to the haunted house. The large wooden doors protected by the crypt keeper seems unusually inviting to her. A shiver crawls up her spine at the thought of going in. She looks back towards Tracy and tries to push the house out of her mind, but something about it pulls at her. She focuses back on Tracy who is sitting at the table, eating her chili dog. Dominique makes herself walk away from the house and sets the beers down on the table and sits down.

"Thanks."

"No problem."

"Do you want to go in?"

"Go in where?"

"The haunted house. I saw you looking at it."

"Oh, no. I think it's interesting, but I'm not interested enough in having the crap scared out of me."

Tracy laughs, "I think it would be kinda fun, but I don't have a big desire to go in right now."

"Good. 'Cause you would have to go in by yourself."

"You wouldn't go in even if I held your hand the whole time?"

Dominique laughs, "You would have to hold more than my hand. I would wrap my body around you like a little kid clinging to safety."

"Hmm, that might not be so bad," Tracy smiles, "Let's go," she pretends like she is going to get up.

Dominique smiles shaking her head. She uses a fork to take a bite of her chili dog, then picks up a napkin to wipe off the left over chili on her face, "There really isn't a graceful way of eating a chili dog, is there?"

"No, not really," she smiles as she picks up a napkin and wipes a spot that Dominique missed.

"Thank you."

Tracy stretches her arms out and yawns, "Man, I'm just exhausted."

"Why don't you see if Jim can handle the clean up. He can always call if he needs you."

"No, I'll wait. I live to far away to get here fast enough if another incident happens, like last night."

"So, stay at my place. I'm ten seconds away."

Tracy, surprised by the invitation says, "Are you sure?"

"Yeah, sure. You're exhausted. You need to get to sleep."

"Ok," she stands up and pulls the radio off of her belt loop, "I'll radio Jim. Be right back," Tracy walks over beside the concession stand, hoping to block some of the blaring band.

Dominique picks up their trash and dumps it in the trash barrel. She looks over at the crowd and spots a familiar face leaning next to the fence separating the concert from the rest of the carnival. A beautiful young woman dressed all in black is staring back at her. Dominique's heart starts to race, as she recognizes the girl from her dream the night before.

* * *

Tracy is wearing jammies she borrowed from Dominique and is nestled on the couch in the living room, drinking a beer.
Dominique is in the bathroom, putting on her jammies and pulling back her hair.

94

"I swear that it was the girl from my dream," Dominique yells from the bathroom.

"Well, you could be psychic, I guess. Except for the part where I'm flirting with her. That's not going to happen."

Dominique walks into the living room, "Well, good. 'Cause I'd have to kick your ass if you did."

Tracy laughs, setting her beer down on the coaster on the coffee table, "Oh, really?"

"Yep."

"You'll have to kick my ass?" she walks to the bathroom and leans against the door frame.

"Well, I figure now would be as good of time as any. You're exhausted and have had a few beers. I'm not that tired and haven't had as many beers."

"I see, you've thought about this?"

"Not really, I'm just quick on my feet," she puts up her dukes and dances like a boxer.

Tracy laughs, "Where do you keep your extra blankets?"

Tracy turns towards the hall closet, where she thinks the extra blankets would be kept. Dominique puts her arms around Tracy's waist.

"I think there are enough blankets on my bed."

Tracy cocks her head to one side and raises her right eyebrow, "You sure? I have no problem sleeping on the couch. I respect your boundaries."

"I know you do," she takes Tracy's hand and pulls her down the hall, flipping off the living room light as they leave the room.

Dominique guides Tracy into the dark bedroom, releases her hand and walks over to her side of the bed and flips on a lamp. Dominique climbs into bed then pats the bed beside her. Tracy closes the bedroom door then lies down beside her. Dominique flips the lamp off and lies back, folding her hands over her stomach. She lies still for a moment then rolls over on her side, facing Tracy. Moonlight seeps between the curtains, leaving a line of light across the center of the bed. Dominique lies there and inspects every feature on Tracy's face. Her heart starts racing as butterflies sprint from her stomach to her throat.

Tracy turns her head to face her, "What?"

Before she can lose the nerve, she blurts out, "I love you."

Tracy's heart melts. She reaches up and brushes the back of her hand across Dominique's cheek, "I love you, too."

Dominique leans over Tracy, pressing her warm body against hers and kisses her, passionately. Tracy returns the kiss; Dominique slides her hand across Tracy's breast, feeling her nipple harden beneath her palm. Tracy wraps her arms around her and rolls her over on her back, putting herself on top of Dominique. Tracy looks down at Dominique, looking in her eyes for a sign to stop or continue. Not getting the stop signal, she pulls off her shirt and tosses it to the floor. The moonlight illumes her firm breasts and Dominique reaches up and touches them tenderly, sending chills throughout Tracy's body. Dominique sits up and pulls off her own shirt, tossing it aside. They look at each other for the first time. Adrenaline pumps through their young solid bodies, each anticipating what will happen next. Dominique wraps her arms around Tracy, pressing their nakedness together, feeling and caressing one another. Tracy kisses Dominique's neck as she gently slides her hands down her back and to her waist. She slides her hand from her stomach to her chest and softly pushes Dominique down. She leans over and kisses her mouth, slow and sweet. She makes her way from her lips to her chin, sliding herself down Dominique's legs; she kisses her between her breasts while gently pulling off Dominique's pj pants. Dominique lifts her waist off the bed so that Tracy can pull the pants the rest of the way off. She climbs back on top of Dominique, straddling her legs over Dominique's leg. She delicately slides her leg against Dominique causing her stomach to sink; she lets out a moan. Tracy slips her hand between her legs and rubs her gently and slowly. Taking Dominique's hand with her free hand, she entwines her fingers between hers, and pulls Dominique's arm above her head. Sliding her hand down her arm, she leans her body closer to Dominique's, pressing herself against her sweating body.

* * *

Dominique and Tracy lie naked in bed, nestled under the covers, enjoying the sun rises. The rays bleed through the mini-blinds into the bedroom, warming the cool crisp air. Tracy wakes up and looks over at Dominique, sleeping so peacefully. She rolls onto her side, facing her lover, and brushes her hair away from her forehead. Dominique breathes in deeply and opens her eyes. She stretches her body awake and smiles up at Tracy.

"Good morning," Tracy says, as she pulls her hand away from Dominique's head.

"Good morning," Dominique responds, intercepting her hand and kissing it.

Dominique pulls Tracy closer and gives her a kiss. Tracy props herself back up on her side and runs her hand through Dominique's hair. She gently traces a faint scar above her eyebrow and below the hair line.

"What's that from?" Tracy asks.

Dominique bites the inside of her lower lip, the way she does when she has to tackle a tough topic, "Prom."

Chapter 14

May, 1996

DOMINIQUE IS SITTING IN FRONT OF HER VANITY PULLING HOT curlers out of her long hair. Her mom, Jade, now at the age of thirty four and as vibrant as she was when she was sixteen, walks in the bedroom and starts to help her remove the curlers.

"You look beautiful. I'm sure you'll be the prom queen."

"I'm sure I won't, Mom. Thanks for the confidence, but that slot is saved for the most popular cheerleader, not for the drama geek."

"Well, the most popular cheerleader did not end up with the quarterback of the football team, now did she? Besides, you are far from geeky."

"Thanks, Mom."

"And, you are far more prettier than Julia, as materialistic as that might sound, it's true."

"Well, I guess I take after you then."

"You're father isn't shabby either."

Dominique looks up at her mom in the mirror and raises her eyebrows at her, she doesn't bring him up very often.

"Well, it's true. He's pretty good looking."

"Yeah, but, you rarely mention him."

"Not my favorite subject, but still, he is good looking," she pulls out the last of the curlers and pulls her hair up off of her neck, putting it in a French twist. Dominique hands her some bobby pins and she fastens it up, leaving tresses of curls flowing from the top.

"There, perfect. What do you think?"

"I don't think he'll recognize me."

Jade walks over to the elegant crimson dress and takes it off the hanger, "Here, stand up."

Dominique stands and gets into her dress. She turns around so that her mom can lace it up. The dress forms to her body, defining her breasts and slender waist. She takes Dominique by the arm and turns her towards the mirror.

"Absolutely breathtaking."

Dominique slips her feet into her heels and takes a look at the complete ensemble, "I guess I look ok."

Jade smacks her in the butt.

"Ok, I look great."

"That's better."

Ding dong!

"Guess he's here. I better get going," Dominique starts to walk out of the room.

"Hey, wait," Jade places a satin shawl around her shoulders and over her arms, "Perfect."

"Thank you," she kisses her on the cheek.

"Be back by midnight, ok?"

"One o'clock?"

"Twelve thirty."

"Deal."

They walk out to the foyer. Jade opens the door. Craig, with his tall, strong, slender frame is wearing black tux pants, a white button up shirt and a crimson tie with matching cummerbund, confidently stands at the door holding a corsage.

"Oh, hello, Mrs. McCloud."

"Ms. McCloud."

"Oh, uh, sorry, Ms. McCloud."

"Come on in. Let me take a picture of you putting on the corsage in the living room."

Jade stands to the side so Craig can come in, allowing him to completely see Dominique.

"Wow, you look amazing," he takes her by the hand and kisses her cheek.

"Thank you. You clean up nicely yourself."

"Oh, this old thing?" he pulls at his jacket.

"Ok, right over here," Jade leads them to the living room in front of the fire place while putting her camera around her neck.

Craig takes the corsage out of the plastic case and places it on the coffee table. He stretches the elastic out to fit it around her wrist.

"Ok, hold it," Jade snaps a picture.

Craig finishes putting it on. Jade snaps more pictures.

"Ok, one more. Pose for me, you know, like a formal picture."

"Mom," Dominique pleads.

"Ah, come on. It's not every day that my only daughter goes to prom."

"Yeah, but, we're going to take pictures at prom too."

"Ah, alright. Get going," She snaps one more picture. Dominique rolls her eyes.

"I'll be home at twelve-thirty."

"Be safe. Love you."

"Love you, too."

They walk out of the house and towards Craig's Camero. He opens the door for her and helps her in. He runs to the other side and slips into the driver's seat.

"You look really good," he looks her up and down, checking out every inch of her.

"Thank you."

He starts the engine and pulls away from the house.

* * *

Craig pulls his car into the packed hotel parking lot. Young men and women are dressed in their formals, walking into the hotel lobby, excited and nervous for what the night might hold. Craig finds a parking spot and helps his date out of the car. They walk to the hotel lobby and step into line behind the rest of the students waiting to have their picture taken. Julia, the captain of the cheerleading squad, pulls out her compact to check her makeup and sees Dominique behind her. She closes the compact and whips around.

"Oh my god, Nickie! You look fabulous! Where did you get that dress?" she greets her with a hint of valley girl in her tone.

"Hey, Julia. Thank you. My mom made it."

"Are you serious? My mom can barely sew on a button!"

Steve, Julia's date and another member of the football team, turns around and shakes Craig's hand.

"Sup, Craig?"

"Sup?"

"I reserved a room to party in later. You two should come up. My dad bought us beer and stuff, it's already in the room," Steve pulls a scrap paper out of his pocket, "Here's the room number."

Craig takes the paper and puts it in his pocket, "Thanks."

"You're dad bought you beer?" Dominique asks him quizzically.

"Yeah, he figures I'm going to drink anyway. He'd rather that we did it in the room and spend the night instead of being out in the orchard and then drive home."

"That's logical, I suppose," Dominique responds while pondering the integrity of Steve's father.

Dominique looks around the ballroom, uninterested in Craig and Steve's un-enlightening conversation about the quantity of alcohol they can drink before vomiting their bowels up. Her eyes stop at Jordan who is standing next to a faux topiary decorated with a string of white lights. Her black formal drapes her delicate frame nicely. The slit that runs from her thigh to her ankle accents her long muscular legs achieved from years of running track. Jordan is unsuccessfully trying to look interested in her date's conversation, as she sips her punch from a plastic cup. Jordan looks amazingly hot, not that she usually isn't attractive, but, oh my god! Dominique catches Jordan's eye with her own, realizing that she was staring at her a little too long. Blushing, she quickly turns her face and looks to see how close they are to taking their picture. Without excusing herself, Jordan starts to walk towards Dominique, right in the middle of some long and boring story Troy was telling.

"Oh, crap," Dominique breathes under her breath.

"Hmmm, did you say something?" Craig asks.

"Oh, no, um, nothing."

"Hey, Dominique. How's it going?" Jordan asks.

"Hey, Jordan. Good. How are you?" Dominique responds, hoping that the blushing has subsided.

"Come on, Dominique. It's our turn," Craig takes her by the hand and leads her towards the backdrop.

Jordan stands to the side as the photographer, an older man wearing a suit that should have stayed in the seventies, starts arranging Craig and Dominique for their prom pose.

"Good, good. Now, boyfriend..."

"He's not my boyfriend," Dominique quickly corrects.

"Uh, ok, then. Young man, put your hand here, around her waist."

"Like this?" Craig asks while gripping her waist.

"Yeah, just a little softer. She's not a football, you know?" Craig eases up his grip.

"Good, good. Now turn your head in a little like this, young lady," the photographer tilts his chin down, striking an over-exaggerated model pose.

"Um, how about like this?" Dominique asks while performing a softer version of his extreme pose.

"It will do. Now don't move. One, two, and..."

Click!

"Perfect, perfect! This will be on your mantel for years to come! Next!"

The photographer pulls the next couple over to the mat, rushing Dominique and Craig out of the way. Jordan walks over to them and takes Dominique by the hand.

"You don't mind if I borrow your date for a minute, do you? I don't want to go to the bathroom alone," Jordan asks.

"No, go ahead. Powder your noses, or whatever. I'll be in there with Steve," Craig points towards the ballroom.

"We'll be back," Jordan responds.

Jordan pulls Dominique through the crowd and into the unusually empty bathroom.

"Must be too early for the bathroom to be crowded, huh?" Dominique states, nervously.

"What was that?" Jordan asks, cornering Dominique between the wall and the counter.

"What was what?" Dominique responds, trying to keep the blushing to a minimum.

"I saw you," Jordan states, accusingly.

"You saw me what?"

"I saw you checking me out!" Jordan stares Dominique down.

Dominique's stomach drops and her heart starts to beat so hard she fears it will pop out her chest.

"I wasn't checking you out! I was just looking at your dress. Black is a really good color for you and the dress is a good style," Dominique quickly tries to explain herself as the temperature rises in her face.

"It's ok," Jordan chuckles as she steps back to give Dominique some space, "I was checking you out when you walked in, too. You look hot."

Dominique looks up at Jordan curiously, not sure what to make of the complement.

"I always wondered if you were," she looks around as if to hide a great secret, "a lesbian. Now I know."

"I'm not..." Dominique starts, but suddenly feels overcome with confusion.

"Oh, come on. It's ok."

Trying to remove the confusion from her mind, "But I'm not. I've never had a 'girlfriend' per say. Nor have I ever kissed a girl. And who's to say that I would want to? I was just looking at your dress." Dominique responds now very defensive.

Jordan walks towards Dominique, cornering her again, and gently presses her body against Dominique's. She leans her face in closer to Dominique's cheek and touches it with hers. Dominique's body reacts, against her will, to Jordan's soft body.

"It's ok if you are because I am. I have always been attracted to you," Jordan whisper's.

She slides her cheek away and looks her in the eye. Dominique relaxes, allowing herself to feel the moment. Her stomach starts to flutter with excitement, a feeling that she has never experienced before. Jordan eases closer and kisses her tenderly on the lips. Dominique melts inside, kissing her back and inviting her tongue to enter her mouth.

Bang!

The bathroom door swings open, hitting the wall behind it.

"Wow, I guess I don't know my own strength," Julia stagers in, laughing.

Dominique quickly pushes away from Jordan as Julia walks the rest of the way in.

"Were you two doing what I think you were doing?" Julia asks, putting her hands on her hips and staring at them with disgust.

"Here you are with the Captain of the football team and you're kissing…her?" Julia's head starts bobbing back and forth faster as she continues to throw her comments at the girls, "Wait until Craig hears about this!"

"Wait a minute! You can't," Dominique, at a loss for words, covers her face with her hands and shakes her head, "Please don't say anything."

"Come on, Julia. Just, be nice for once in your life and don't ruin her and Craig's night. It was my fault," Jordan states, taking all the blame, "I kissed her, she didn't kiss me."

Dominique looks over at Jordan, confused.

Julia looks at them both, silent for a moment, "Fine, but let's go, now, Dominique," Julia takes Dominique by the hand and pulls her out of the bathroom.

"I can't believe you. You're not a lesbian," Julia spouts out loud enough for only Dominique to hear, "You didn't like it, did you?"

"I…" Dominique starts, leaning more on the liking it rather than the not. Before she has to answer, Craig walks up to them.

"There you are. You were in the bathroom forever. I want to dance. Come on," Craig leads Dominique onto the dance floor.

Julia walks over to Steve who is sitting at a table sneaking drinks from his flask. She sits down next to him and takes the flask from him.

"Did you save me any?"

"There's plenty and if there's not, we just go up to the room and fill it up."

Julia takes a quick swig and hands it back, "You're not going to believe what I just saw in the girls' bathroom!"

Steve rolls his eyes, "Here we go with the gossip. Who's kissing whose boyfriend?"

"Close. Try which girls are kissing each other."

Steve quickly tightens the lid on the flask and places it in his jacket, "What?"

"I just caught Jordan kissing Dominique."

"No way! I don't believe it," Steve responds while looking over at Dominique and Craig getting ready to dance to a slow song, "That's hot!"

Julia hits his arm, "Perv!"

Jordan walks into the ballroom and looks around for Troy who is busily talking to whoever will listen to him. She walks over to his table and taps him on the shoulder.

"Dance with me."

"Yes, ma'am," Troy obediently gets out of his seat.

Jordan leads him over to the dance floor, near Dominique and Craig. She puts her arms around Troy's shoulders as he places his hands on her hips.

"Let's dance," Steve stands up from his seat and puts his hand out for Julia who accepts it.

"Let's."

Steve guides his date next to Dominique and Craig. He wraps his arms around Julia making it look as if they are hugging more than dancing. Julia places her head on Steve's shoulder, allowing him to hold her up after her several drinks from the flask.

"I feel so, light."

"Not to me you don't," Steve jokes.

Julia smacks him on the shoulder, "How rude!"

"Oh, I'm kidding. When this song is over, you want to go up to the room?"

"Sure. I need to get out of these shoes."

"Cool. I'll let Craig know too," Steve states right when the song ends.

Julia releases Steve as he walks over to Craig.

"Hey, we're going upstairs. You want to come with?"

"Yeah, sounds good to me. Do you care?" Craig asks Dominique.

"Oh, no, that's fine."

"Cool. Could you help me out with something first, Craig? In the lobby?"

"Yeah, sure," he tells Craig then turns to Dominique, "I'll meet you by the elevator, ok?"

"Ok."

Craig, Steve, and Julia walk out of the ballroom while Dominique tries to quickly find Jordan. Jordan and Troy have already made it back to their table sitting with another couple. Dominique walks over to the table and sits in an empty chair in front of Jordan.

"Hey, are you all leaving?" Jordan asks.

"No, we're going up to Steve's room. His dad rented a room. You all should come up too."

"Sound's cool," Troy responds, "How about a few more dances, then we go?"

"Ok," Jordan responds, shrugging her shoulders.

Dominique leans over to Jordan and whispers in her ear, "You know it wasn't all you, right? I loved it," Dominique stands up, placing her hand on Jordan's leg for leverage.

Jordan looks up at her and smiles as she watches Dominique walk out of the ballroom. Like a scene from a movie, she replays the kiss in her mind.

Craig is already at the elevator, waiting for Dominique; she picks up her pace.

"Ready?" Craig asks while pressing the call button.

"Sure."

"What were you doing?"

"I was just inviting a few more people up."

"Oh, that's cool."

The elevator chimes and the door opens. He steps to the side, holding the door open for Dominique, and then steps in beside her.

He presses the button to the third floor, "Who did you invite?"

"Troy and Jordan. I figured it would be ok since Troy's on the team."

"Troy's cool. He talks a lot, but he's cool."

The elevator comes to a stop and the doors open. Craig steps out of the elevator and holds it open. Dominique steps out and adjusts her shawl around her shoulders, wrapping it close to her exposed shoulders. Craig leads the way down the hall and pulls an access card from his pocket. He walks up to room three-o-six and slips the card into the reader. The door unlocks and he pushes it open for Dominique. She peers into the empty room then takes a step back.

"Where is everyone? I thought this was the party room."

"Oh, we'll meet up with them later. I got this room for us, I thought we could have our own private party first."

"I don't think that's a good idea. Where's the other room?" Dominique asks as she turns to head down the hallway.

Craig grabs her elbow and pulls her close to him, "Come on. Just a couple of drinks. All I want to do is talk. We never get to talk and if we are in a crowded room, how will we get to know each other?"

Dominique lets her guard down, "Ok, just a few drinks. I could really use a soda."

"Good, come in," Dominique follows him in the room, "I believe I have your favorite soda ready for you," he points at the cans of Pepsi lined up on the dresser sitting beside a bottle of Jack Daniels.

Surprised at his attention to detail, "Pepsi? I didn't think you paid that close of attention."

"Why, of course. This is our senior year – our last prom, I wanted it to be perfect," he picks up a cup and fills it with ice.

Dominique pops open a can of soda, "Thank you," she says, taking the cup from him.

"You sure you don't want a little Jack in that soda?" he asks, wiggling the bottle of whiskey in front of her.

"Well, I guess, a little."

"Here, give me your cup. Sit down, relax. I'll bring it to you," he takes the cup from her and gently pushes her towards the bed.

She sits on the end of the bed and kicks off her heals, "God, that feels good," she sits farther back on the bed and pulls her feet up so she can rub them.

Craig brings over the drink and hands it to her. He kicks his shoes off and sits down next to her. He takes her feet and starts to rub them.

"Oh, you don't have to do that. But it does feel good."

"No problem. I don't mind."

Craig continues to rub her feet. Dominique leans back against the head board and takes a long drink.

"Mmmm, this is good. I've never had one before."

"Are you serious? You've never had alcohol before?"

"I've had champagne and wine, on special occasions. But usually just a sip for a toast."

"Oh, well, welcome to the world of Jack and Pepsi. Much better tasting, if you ask me."

"I agree, absolutely."

Craig inches his body closer to hers and works his hands from her feet to her calves.

"How does that feel?"

"Actually, kinda uncomfortable," she pulls her legs away from him and tucks them under her butt. She sets her drink on the side table, "So, are we going to meet up with Steve and Julia now?"

"Well," he pushes himself up on his knees and sits in front of her, "I was thinking that you might want to do other things."

She tries to shimmy back from him, but is greeted by the thud of the headboard against the wall. Craig picks up a remote sitting on the nightstand and clicks on the TV. He turns it up loud.

"Come on, let's go. I'm not ready for this," Dominique tries to get up but is barricaded by Craig's body.

Craig leans in and tries to kiss her. Dominique turns her head so that he kisses her cheek.

"Ah, come on, just a kiss," Craig tries again.

"Stop it! I don't like you like that!" she tries to push him away.

"So, what? You only like chicks like that? Are you a fuckin' dyke or what?"

"What?"

"Oh, I heard about you and Jordan in the bathroom. Did you think it wouldn't get around?"

"Let's just go to the party," she tries to get around him and scoot off the bed.

Craig pushes her up against the headboard and kisses her neck.

"Stop! Stop!"

He cups his hand over her breast and brushes his thumb over her nipple. She gets her arm free and pushes him on his back. She jumps off the bed and runs towards the door. Craig jumps off the bed and catches her before she reaches it. He grabs her by the arm, swinging her around towards him. He backhands her across the face splitting the skin above her eyebrow, making her to bleed then throws her on the bed.

"Help!" she screams from the top of her lungs, but the sound becomes intermingled with the noise from the TV.

Craig jumps on top of her, covering her mouth with his hand and pinning her arms with his legs.

* * *

Jordan and Troy walk down the hall towards room three-twenty-nine. Julia walks out of the room, drink in hand.

"Hey, you two. Come on in. Have a drink. Have two drinks, have as many drinks as you want!" she laughs at herself then starts to fall back. Troy reaches out and steadies her.

"Looks like you've had a few," Troy points out.

"A few and I will have a few more. Come in!" she leads them into the room.

A blood curdling scream fills the hall, masked by loud music coming from one end of the hall and a blaring TV from the other.

"Did you hear that?" Jordan asks before stepping into the room.

"Hear what?" Julia asks, falling over herself.

Jordan puts her hand out to shush Julia. She listens intently for another scream, but does not hear one.

"Must have been part of the song," she shrugs her shoulders and walks into the room.

* * *

Dominique bites down hard on Craig's hand. He rips his hand away and yelps in pain.

"Bitch!" he pulls his fist back.

"Nooooooo!" she screams while turning her cheek.

His fist slams into her temple sending an explosion through her head. She gasps in pain. Her world starts spinning and her body grows weak. Craig, taking advantage of her disorientation, pulls her dress up around her waist and rips her panty hose off. He slides her undies down and flips them aside.

"All you need is a little beef. That'll take care of your issues!" he tosses his cummerbund aside and unzips his pants.

Dominique starts to reorient herself. She sees him pulling out his penis; she quickly sits up on the bed, trying to steady herself after the blow to her head.

With her voice cracking, she tries to yell, "Help me," but the words barely leave her lips before she is slammed back on the bed. She flips over and tries to crawl away from him.

"Oh, that's right. You might like it that way," he grabs her by the waist and drags her into him.

She clings onto the bedspread, dragging it with her as he pulls her. He grabs his staff and plunges it into her. She gasps in pain as the hard rod forces its way into her virginity. He thrusts himself into her, harder, faster, harder, faster. She rests her head on the mattress, trying to wish herself away from that place. Tears stream down her face. She tries to find her voice.

"Someone, please help," the words cross her mind, but never make it out of her mouth.

"God, yeah!" he slams himself into her a couple more times then grabs tightly to her waist as he releases his fluids into her, "Fuck, yeah," he pulls himself out of her and grabs her shawl from the bed. He wipes himself with it and tosses it aside.

Dominique falls over on her side and pulls her legs up to her chest. She pulls the comforter over her body and lies, motionless. Craig finishes pulling up his pants and walks towards the door.

"C'ya, bitch," he opens the door and leaves.

Dominique lies there for a moment, trying to shut out what had just happened to her. She looks over at the nightstand and stares at the phone. Using all her strength, she pulls herself towards it and picks up the receiver. She dials a number and places the phone to her ear.

"Hello?" the sweet voice of salvation answers the phone.

Struggling to get words to leave her mouth, "Momma? Could you come get me?"

"Nickie? What's wrong, baby?"

"Please come get me. I'm in room three-o-six," tears stream down her cheeks.

"What happened? What's wrong?"

"Just come, please."

"I'll be there in fifteen minutes."

Click.

* * *

Craig walks down the hall, tucking in his shirt, towards Steve's room. The door is partially propped open. He swings the door open and loudly walks into the room.

"Hey! What's going on?" he walks in, slapping hands with some of his buddies.

Jordan walks over to him, "Where's Dominique?"

"Wouldn't you like to know, dyke?" he takes a beer out of an ice filled tub and pops off the top.

Jordan points to the blood stain on his bright white shirt, "What the fuck is that?"

"Damn, the bitch bled on me!" he brushes his shirt off, transferring more blood on it from his bleeding hand.

"Where is she?" she steps up and gets in his face.

"Down the hall. Here," he takes the access card from his pocket and throws it at her, "If you like sloppy seconds, she's waiting," he laughs at himself.

Jordan picks the card off the floor, "You son-of-a-bitch."

"Whatever," he takes a swig from his beer and walks over to a group of his buddies.

Jordan runs out of the room down the hall. She goes by each door, sticking the access card into each one until the right door opens up. She pushes the door open and is greeted by the loud TV. She slowly walks into the room, clicking off the TV as passes by it. She sees Dominique lying on the bed, still covered with the blanket.

"Dominique! What happened?" Jordan rushes over to the bed and sits down beside her. She reaches out to move her hair away from her face; Dominique winces.

"Oh my god, what did he do to you?" she gets off the bed and rushes into the bathroom. She takes a washcloth from the rack and runs back towards the bed and places it on Dominique's bleeding head, "What happened?"

Dominique starts crying again. She should have walked out the door when she saw it wasn't the party room. Her gut told her too, why didn't she listen to her gut?

Bang! Bang! Bang!

"Nickie! Are you in there?"

Jordan jumps off the bed and opens the door. Jade pushes her way past Jordan and into the room. She rushes to the bed and sits down next to Dominique.

"What the hell happened?" Jade demands while sitting next to her daughter.

Dominique puts her head on her mom's leg and holds on to her.

"I don't know. All I know is that Craig came back to the room with blood on his shirt without Dominique. I rushed over here and found her like this."

Jade tenderly pulls Dominique's hair back, revealing the developing bruises on her face. She reaches over and picks up the phone and dials 911.

"911. What's your emergency?"

"My daughter has been raped," Jade states, her voice cracking as the truth is stated aloud.

"I show that you are calling from the Radisson. I have a unit on the way. Which room?"

"Three-o-six."

"Is the perpetrator still in the building?"

Jade looks over at Jordan, "Is that bastard still in the hotel?"

"Yeah, down the hallway."

"He's here," Jade states to the operator.

"What's the victim's name?"

Jade's skin crawls at the thought of her daughter being the victim, "Dominique McCloud."

The operator types some notes. It feels like an eternity before she comes back on the line.

"I have word that the unit is there. I'm going to let you go now."

"Ok," Jade hangs up the phone.

Jordan opens the door and sees the EMT's making their way down the hall with a gurney. She steps aside, holding the door open for them.

"Is this the room?" asks the EMT.

"Yes, ma'am," Jordan answers, pressing her body against the wall so they can get in.

The EMT's rush into the room. Jordan starts to close the door when she sees two police officers walking down the hall towards the room.

"Hello," Officer Jones walks up to Jordan, "Do you know what happened?"

"My friend was raped by her prom date."

"Who's her date?" Officer Jones asks while pulling a notepad out from his pocket.

"Craig Fletcher."

Officer Jones looks at his partner and jots the name down in his book.

"The quarterback, Craig Fletcher?" Officer Jones asks.

"The one and the same," Jordan responds.

"Ok, well, is he still here?"

"Yeah, he's down the hall in another room. I can take you there."

"Ok. Officer Bernardo, go with her to the other room. I'll work on getting a statement."

"Sure thing."

Officer Jones goes into the room. Jordan starts walking down the hall.

"This way."

Officer Bernardo follows her down the corridor, a few rooms down to party central. Jordan walks up to the cracked door and gets ready to open it.

"I'll get it. You can go back down to the other room, if you'd like. I don't want you to get hurt if he becomes violent."

"Ok, no problem."

Jordan backs away from the door and watches the officer walk into the room.

"Bernardo! What the heck are you doing here?" Troy asks his ex-teammate.

"I'm afraid this is official business," he looks over at Craig, who is completely drunk, "I need you to come with me."

"But I wasn't driving, officer," Craig makes light of the situation.

"Come on, now. I don't want any trouble."

Craig stands up from the chair and walks over to Officer Bernardo, "What seems to be the problem?"

"Why don't you step outside with me?" Officer Bernardo puts his hand on his shoulder to guide him out.

Craig slips out from under his hand and steps back, "There's nothing you can't say in front of my friends. It's not like I've done anything wrong."

"Well, ok," he pulls his handcuffs out from his holster, "You're under arrest."

Craig laughs, "Yeah right, Bernardo, for what?"

"For the rape of Dominique McCloud. You have the right to remain silent," he takes Craig's left arm and puts the handcuffs on, then pulls it behind his back.

"You have got to be kidding me, I didn't do anything she didn't want."

"If you give up this right, anything you say can and will be held against you in a court of law," he finishes cuffing the other arm.

"Steve, call my dad. He'll take care of this."

Officer Bernardo escorts Craig out of the room as Steve picks up the hotel phone and starts dialing.

* * *

The hospital is relatively quiet for a Saturday night. The halls are usually crowded with homeless folks trying to get a warm space to sleep for the night by suddenly developing an illness so they can be seen. At least they are given the chance to warm up before being sent on their way. And, if they are lucky, they might be able to get a free sandwich and soda. Nurses are walking around the halls performing miscellaneous duties to make the time pass while a couple of doctors work on their rounds. Officer Jones is sitting outside a closed curtain writing a few notes when a nurse walks over to him.

"Officer. You have a call at the nurses' station."

Officer Jones nods in understanding and walks over to the nurses' station, "Officer Jones here," he pauses and listens for a moment, "I will let them know," he hangs up the phone and walks back over towards Dominique's room.

A nurse pulls the curtain back, letting herself out of the exam area with her specimens. Officer Jones walks into the exam area. Dominique's face has been cleaned up, a couple of stitches have been placed over her right eye. Jade is standing next to her, holding her hand.

"Well, he has made bail."

"What? He was given bail?" Jade asks, astonished.

"Well, this was a first offence not to mention that his judgment was impaired due to being inebriated. The judge allowed it."

115

"The judge only allowed it because he is Martin Fletcher's son and the quarterback of the football team. They should not be treated as if they are above the law!"

"You have the right to obtain a restraining order. He will not be allowed to come within one hundred feet of Dominique."

"He better not come within one foot of my daughter!"

"I know you are upset, Ms. McCloud. But don't go sounding like you are going to do something to that boy or I'll have to take measures."

Jade sighs, pissed off, "Are you serious? That jackass does this to my little girl, gets out on bail, and you are going to have to take measures against me? Are you done?"

"Just about. All I need is for Dominique to sign this statement," he hands her a clipboard and pen, "This just states the details of the night."

Dominique signs it and hands it back to him.

"Goodnight, and I'm sorry this happened to you," Officer Jones states sincerely as he leaves the room.

"Can we go now? I just want to go to bed."

"I know, honey. We just have to wait for the doctor to come back. Let me see where he is," Jade steps out from behind the curtain, "He's coming."

Dr. Jepson takes Dominique's file from its slot in the wall. He walks in beside her and flips through the chart.

"Your CT scan came back normal so no permanent damage to the brain, just a concussion. The nurse has taken swabs and they will be analyzed verifying that the DNA matches that of the perp. I'm going to have the nurse bring you a pill called the PCP, post-coital pill, otherwise known as the morning after pill. This will help stop the possibility of becoming pregnant. It's not one hundred percent effective, but pretty close, in my experience. There are some uncommon side effects such as stomachache, headache, spotting, breast tenderness, and dizziness. Your next period may come early, or late, but if it is more than a couple of days past when your period should have come, see your physician. Any questions?"

"No," Dominique states.

"Ok. I will sign your discharge papers and the nurse will bring the pill in to you," he states while signing the forms.

"Thank you, Doctor," Jade states, graciously.

"You are very welcome," he sincerely responds as he leaves.

Jordan walks in holding two cups of coffee. She hands one to Jade and takes a sip from the other.

"Thank you so much," Jade politely takes the cup from Jordan.

"Thank you for staying," Dominique tries to choke back her tears.

"Oh, no problem," she tenderly takes Dominique's hand and brushes her thumb across the top of it.

Jade walks over to Jordan and places her hand on her arm, "Yes, thank you for staying. You've already done so much, but could you possibly do one more thing for us?"

"Sure, anything," Jordan replies.

"Could you stay at our house with Nickie while I run an errand? I want to get her prescriptions filled and I don't want her to have to wait at home by herself."

"Yeah, absolutely. Not a problem."

"Do you need to call your mom or anything?"

"Yeah, I better," Jordan lets go of Dominique's hand and walks out of the room.

Nurse Edna, walks into the room with the discharge papers and a pair of scrubs and slipper socks. She sets the clothes on the bed.

"I thought you might want to change," Nurse Edna hands her a paper cup, "Go ahead and take this," she takes a cup of water on the table next to her and hands it to her.

Dominique does as she is told and then hands the cups back to the nurse, "Thank you for the scrubs."

"No problem, darling. Here are your discharge papers. The prescriptions are attached," she hands Jade the papers, pointing out the prescription section as she does so.

Nurse Edna nods at Dominique then leaves the room. Jade folds the papers and puts them in her purse. She picks up the scrubs and walks in front of her daughter. She pulls the bow holding the gown together allowing it to slip off her delicate body. The bruises around her waist have blackened in the shape of fingers. Jade tentatively touches her waist. She grows increasingly angry as she thinks of what happened to Nickie, her baby, shaking her head in disgust, tears start to stream down her face. She puts the scrub shirt over her head; Dominique sticks her arms through. Jordan walks back in, sipping her coffee.

Jade quickly wipes the tears from her eyes, "Jordan, could you drive her home. I'm just going to leave from here, if that's ok with you," she looks at Dominique.

"That's fine, Mom. The sooner you go, the sooner you get home."

"Exactly," she grabs the plastic laundry bag containing her prom dress and her purse, "Ok, sweetie, I'll see you at home," she kisses the top of her head.

"Ok."

* * *

Jordan walks into Dominique's room wearing lavender satin pajama pants and a tank top. She has a towel on her head, trying to squeeze all of the water out from her shower. Dominique is lying in bed, hugging her body pillow, deep under her covers. Jordan sets the towel down over the back of the chair in front of her desk then sits down next to Dominique on the bed.

"Thank you for letting me borrow your pj's. I just needed to get out of that dress."

"You're welcome."

Jordan sits silently, trying to figure out what to say to her hurting friend, but nothing she can think of quite fits the situation.

Dominique looks up at Jordan, sensing her awkwardness she says, "I wouldn't know what to say either."

Jordan looks down at Dominique, "You are an amazingly strong woman," she brushes Dominique's hair out of her face and tucks it behind her ear.

Dominique smiles at her, "We'll see."

"I can't imagine," she stops herself, "I'm so sorry."

"You didn't do it. I just can't believe I trusted him when everything in my being told me not to. I need to learn to trust my gut," she clenches her jaw, trying not to cry again.

"How could you have known this would happen? Don't beat yourself up for this. Beat him up for this."

"Castration seems like a good option."

"I completely agree."

Jordan leans over on her arm and yawns. She covers her mouth and looks at the clock, three in the morning, "Sorry."

"You can lie down, if you want," Dominique looks over at the empty spot beside her and pulls back the blankets.

"Oh, ok," she flips herself around, shimmy's under the covers and lies on her back, "Nice stars," she points to the glow-in-the-dark plastic stars stuck to the ceiling.

"Thanks. I like them."

Jordan takes a deep breath, "This might not be something you want to talk about, and, if you don't, tell me, but I'm sorry I kissed you in the bathroom," she lets out her breath.

Dominique looks over at Jordan and gently touches her arm, "Don't be. That was the best part of my night."

Jordan turns over on her side and looks at Dominique, "Well, I'm not sure what to think about that since you had a very shitty night."

"I just want to forget about that, please, let's just forget about it. All I want to remember of my Senior prom is how I was kissed by the most beautiful girl in school," Dominique blushes at her directness.

Jordan smiles, "That's what I want to remember, too. God, I've had a crush on you for so long."

"Really?"

"Hell yeah! Then when I saw you walk into the lobby in that dress, very beautiful dress by the way, I couldn't resist. I had to kiss you."

Dominique smiles, but it fades quickly. Tears start pouring down her face, uncontrollably, "I can't stop thinking about it."

"Oh, sweetheart," Jordan hugs her tight.

* * *

Jade walks into the kitchen and sets her purse down on the counter next to the microwave, the clock reads four o'clock. She pulls out a white pharmacy bag from her purse and takes out the bottle of Vicoden. She puts some ice in a cup and fills it with filtered water and heads down the hall to Dominique's room. A bedside lamp dimly lights up the room. Dominique is sleeping with her head on Jordan's chest; Jordan has her arm around her and has long since fallen asleep. Jade walks over to Dominique's side of the bed and puts the glass down and sets a pill next to it. She leans over the bed and kisses Dominique on the back of her head then clicks off the lamp and walks out of the room.

* * *

A tear rolls down Dominique's cheek as she relives the horrors of that night to Tracy. Tracy kisses the tear off her cheek and hugs her tight.

"I am so sorry. I'm glad you had Jordan," she rolls back over onto her arm.

"Yeah, me too. And my mom. My mom has always been my strength. We are more like best friends than mother and daughter. She was so young when she had me, we practically grew up together."

"How old was she?"

"Sixteen, almost seventeen."

Tracy lies there for a moment, taking in everything she had just heard. She sits up and crosses her legs, pulling the blankets up around her to conceal her nakedness.

"Did he get jail time?"

"No."

"Are you serious? His bullshit popularity got him off?"

"No. He never had that opportunity. He was killed by a wolf or some kind of animal. The coroner could never tell what kind of animal it was. They found his body in the middle of the football field that night. He'd been drinking. They think he passed out, which is when the animal got him."

"Well, good. That son-of-a-bitch deserved it."

Chapter 15

May, 1996

JADE RUSHES THROUGH THE HOSPITAL PARKING LOT, GETS
into her VW bug and starts the engine. Tears have removed any
sign of mascara that once covered her eyelashes. Pounding on the
steering wheel, she screams at the top of her lungs, the excruciating
pain of a breaking heart fills the car. She slams the shifter into
reverse and races out of the parking space. Putting the car into
first, she pushes the gas pedal to the floor and peels out of the
parking lot. She can barely see through the tears as she makes her
way down the road, down a once familiar path. As if by fate, every
light is green as she makes her way through town towards the
country. The stars hang bright in the dark sky as she leaves the land
of street lights and civilization towards the country. She flips her
high beams on and forges ahead, wiping her tears as she gets closer
to her turn. She slows the car and takes a left down the long gravel

drive up to the castle where she conceived Dominique. She pulls in front of the walk way, opening the door before she turns the car off. She leaves the door open and the keys in the car then runs up to the front door. Steadying herself before she enters the house, she places her hands on her knees and takes a deep breath. She lifts the knocker and lets it fall, banging loudly on the massive wooden door. The door swings open, a slender woman in an evening gown holding a glass of champagne opens the door.

"Can I help you?" she asks with a French accent.

Jade walks past her, "I'm looking for Shadow."

The French woman gasps, "Excuse you, you were not invited in."

Jade spins around and stares her in the eye, "Step off, bitch."

"There's nothing more dangerous than a woman scorned," Sabin states, walking down the stairs in his jeans and half buttoned up white shirt.

"It's ok, Francesca, she's an old friend," Sabin states, stepping off the last step and walking up to Jade.

Francesca turns and walks away.

"And to what do we owe this honor?"

"I need you and Shadow to take care of something."

Sabin puts his hand on her back and leads her down the hall to the sitting room, "And why, might I ask, should we want to do anything for you?"

"It's not just for me. It's for Nickie as well."

"Ewww, I hate that nickname, Nickie. Please, call her by her Christian name."

Jade shakes her head, "Christian, that's funny coming from you."

Sabin shrugs his shoulders, "I didn't make up the saying," he guides her over to an overstuffed leather chair and motions for her to sit.

"I can't sit! I'm too pissed! Where's Shadow?"

"He's right there," Sabin points to the doorway at Shadow as he takes a seat.

Shadow's face softens with compassion at the sight of his one love. He walks in the room and up to Jade. Jades' eyes well up at the sight of him, her heart melts at the remembrance of his touch;

123

how safe she once felt with him. Tears flow freely from her eyes as she allows herself to fall into his arms.

"Dominique was raped," she sobs.

"What!" Sabin shouts, jumping to his feet.

"By whom?" Shadow asks, holding her tight.

"Craig Fletcher. And they say he's going to get away with it because his 'judgment was impaired due to alcohol'," she replies, stepping back from Shadow, "You know I would never come to you if I wasn't desperate. I want you to take care of this," She wipes her tears and puts her guard back up.

"Of course," Shadow replies.

"That's the quarterback, right?" Sabin asks.

"Yes."

"Yummy, he's a cutie," Sabin replies, seductively, "Shadow, why don't you show Jade out. Rest assured that we will take care of this, tonight."

Jade nods at Sabin in appreciation. Shadow guides Jade out of the room. They walk in silence to the front door and out to the car.

"I..." Shadow starts.

"I..." Jade interrupts, trying to hold in her emotions.

"Go ahead," Shadow insists.

"I miss you. I miss how you make me feel, safe, and secure."

"I miss you too. I have never loved anyone the way I love you," he wipes the tears off her cheek.

"Me neither."

Shadow puts his arms around her, holding her tight against his firm chest, "It's not too late. We can still be together."

Jade hugs him back, squeezing him tight, then lets him go, "I can't," she gets into her car and drives away.

* * *

Halogen lights brighten up the dark football field. Craig and Steve are sitting on the hood of Steve's truck, downing cheap beer and laughing like fools. The night sky is being over taken by clouds carrying moisture over the small town. Lightening intensifies the night in the distance while a slight rumble of thunder rolls over them.

"Well, shit, man. It's gonna rain on us if we don't get outta here," Steve states, slurring.

"Yeah, you go on home. I'm gonna walk."

"You sure?"

"Yeah, go ahead. My buzz is starting to wear off anyway."

"Alright."

They slide off the hood and toss the beer cans into the bed.

"I'm glad you're out of jail, man. Even though it was a short stint in the joint, it seemed like an eternity," Steve holds a straight face momentarily then lets out a loud laugh.

"Yeah, dude, I know what you mean."

Steve jumps into his truck and starts it up, "See ya later."

"Yeah, see ya."

Steve's redneck truck rumbles out of the stadium and down the street. Sprinkles come down and land on Craig. He looks up at the sky and puts his arms out, palms up, inviting the rain onto his body.

"Rain is great, isn't it?" Sabin asks, walking up behind Craig.

Craig turns around, his heart racing, "What the fuck, dude? You scared the shit out of me."

Sabin shrugs his shoulders, "Ah, come on now. You didn't think you were out here all by yourself, did you?"

"I gotta go," Craig turns around and starts walking across the field.

"Ah, come on, I'm sorry I scared you. Stay," Sabin follows him.

Craig whips around to face him, "No offence, man, but I'm not your kind of guy."

"And what kind of guy is that?"

"Faggot, fudge packer, queer, whatever you guys call yourselves these days."

"Ah, I see."

"So, what do you like?"

"I like pussy, man, back off. Go find someone else," Craig turns around and picks up his pace. He takes a step, then, like lightening, Sabin steps in front of him.

"You kiss your mom with that mouth?"

"Shut up."

"So, you only like girls. Like the one you raped?"

"How, the? Ah, I've had one too many. I don't know what you are talking about," he tries to walk around him, but Sabin blocks him.

"You know, the girl you raped tonight, Dominique," he stares him in the eye.

"It was consensual."

"Oh, was it?" he rubs the stubble on his chin, "You see, I don't think it happened that way."

"You know what buddy, I'm this close from knocking you on your ass. Now, get the fuck out of my way," he puts his hand up and motions with his thumb and forefinger the small distance of which he was ready to pounce Sabin.

Sabin grabs his hand to look closer at the bite mark Dominique left on him, "Hmmm, she bit you. Good girl. Looks like she got some blood out of you too," he licks his lips.

Craig pulls his hand away from him, "Freak!"

Sabin looks up at the goal post and nods at Shadow, who is sitting perched on top wearing a trench coat. Craig looks in the direction Sabin is and sees Shadow stand up on the post.

"How in the hell did he get up there?"

"You see, I'm Dominique's uncle and that guy there, that's her father. And you, my friend, made a terrible mistake when you decided to rape our little girl."

Shadow freefalls from the goal post and flies towards Craig. Craig's eyes widen in terror as he runs in the opposite direction. Sabin watches him run as Shadow increasingly approaches Craig.

"You might want to run faster than that, quarterback. He's gonna get you!" he yells, laughing.

Craig looks over his shoulder and tries to pick up the pace. Shadow swoops down and scoops Craig up off the ground. Craig lets out a scream as urine runs down his leg.

"We've got a pisser," Shadow yells down to Sabin, then sinks his teeth into his neck.

"Save some for me, brother."

Shadow nods at him. Craig passes out as Shadow flies away with him. Rain starts pouring down.

* * *

Behind the dark wine cellar lies a dungeon in the DeFleur castle. Torches line the rock walls in between metal cages furnished with a hole in the ground for relieving oneself. In the center of the room is a stainless steel examination table. Leather restraints are affixed to the sides and at the bottom of the table. A pull down shower handle, like the ones used in a mortician's autopsy room, dangles above the table. There are no windows to be found in this sound proof crypt, and only one obvious way out.

Shadow makes his way down the dark corridor with Craig thrown over his shoulder like a sack of potatoes. He walks over to the autopsy table and lies him down on his back. The blood on his neck has coagulated and is starting to scab over, his breathing is shallow, but he is breathing. Shadow slips the restraints on Craig's wrists and ankles then rips his shirt off of him, shredding it, and tosses it in the corner. Craig starts to groan, awakening from his slumber. Shadow grabs the ankle of Craig's jeans and rips them from ankle to waist. He wrinkles his nose at the stench of drying urine. Quickly trying to finish the task, he rips one last strip and throws the pants to the side.

Craig groans again and starts to open his eyes. He blinks heavily, trying to figure out where he is. He turns his head to the left, then the right. Shadow pulls the nozzle down from above Craig and starts to rinse him off.

"Oh my god! What are you doing!" he shivers under the cold water.

"I don't like dirty meat."

Suddenly he realizes that he can't move. He looks down at his arms and legs and tries to pull himself free.

"Don't bother, you're not getting out of here, shrivel dick," he squirts his penis with the cold water.

"Oh, come on, Shadow, that's not very eloquent of you," Sabin states as he approaches the table.

Shadow rinses Craig's neck and hair, then let's go of the nozzle. It retracts up by the spring suspending it to the ceiling and swings back and forth.

"What are you going to do to me?" Craig asks, spitting water out of his mouth.

"Ravage you - cause you the pain that you caused my daughter, with one exception, you get to actually die rather than just feeling dead inside."

"What? I swear, guys, I didn't do anything. Is it money you want? My dad has lots of money. I can call him right now and he'll wire it to any account you want, no questions asked, just let me go," he pleads.

Sabin stretches his arms out and looks around the room, "Does it look like we need money? Do you have a room like this in your house?" he chuckles, "Daddy isn't going to be able to get you out of this one."

Sabin and Shadow smile down at Craig, revealing their fangs.

"What the hell are you?" tears start to form in his eyes.

"What do you think we are?" Shadow asks.

"Vam...Vampires," he stutters.

Shadow claps his hands, "Good job. He does have a brain."

"Indeed."

Craig starts whimpering uncontrollably, "What can I do to fix this?" he asks between whimpers.

"What do you think you could do to fix this? Give Dominique back her virginity?" Shadow growls between his teeth, "You know, boy, I don't usually like to take the life from humans."

"It's true, he doesn't," Sabin acknowledges, sincerely.

"But, for you, I will make an exception. But first, I would like for you to meet a few of my guests," he looks down the hall at a group of vampires walking toward them, "This is Sedrick, he likes young boys..."

"Oooh, don't forget that I like young boys too," Sabin pipes in, raising his hand, prancing on his tip toes.

"Of course not, brother, you get him first."

"What do you mean 'he gets me first'?"

"Silence!" Shadow yells, striking him across the face with the back of his hand, "I'm not finished with introductions."

"Oh, we don't need to be introduced. Why don't you just tell him what he has to look forward to," Sedrick replies.

"I see that my guests are eager. I don't like to keep them waiting, so I shall proceed as requested," he bends down over Craig, putting his mouth near his ear, "My brother is going to rape you and when he is done, Sedrick is going to rape you. And while this is going on, I will drink the blood from your neck while the rest of my guests feed on whatever part of your body they want to. Once they are done, we will toss your filthy body back in the football stadium where we found you."

Sabin starts to unzip his pants and walk to the foot of the table. Craig starts to cry uncontrollably.

"Shhh," Shadow puts his finger over Craig's lips, "When they find your body, they will barely recognize you. They will think you were attacked by animals after you passed out from drunkenness," he nods at Sherry who is holding a bottle of Jack Daniels, "This is your favorite, isn't it? I tasted it in your blood."

Sherry lifts the bottle and twists off the cap. Sedrick holds Craig's head up and Sherry pours the liquid down his throat. Craig coughs from it going down the wrong pipe, but she keeps on pouring.

"Swallow!" Shadow demands.

Craig does as he is told. When she thinks she has given him enough, she places the bottle on a nearby table.

Shadow stands up straight and looks at his brother, then at his guests, "Bon appetite!"

Shadow stands back as the guests circle him, like vultures coming in for their kill. Sabin un-straps his ankles; Sedrick and Sherry un-strap his arms. Sabin pulls Craig down to the edge of the table and nods to the other guests to hold his legs. Craig struggles against them, but is no match to their superhuman strength.

Shadow tosses Sabin a bottle of lubricant, he rubs some on and then walks up to Craig, "All you need is a little beef, right?" he pushes himself in him.

Craig gasps in breathtaking pain. Sabin holds on to Craig's legs, giving him adequate leverage, then nods at the rest, permitting them to do with him whatever they please.

Craig's screams echo down the corridor as the guests feast upon his flesh.

Chapter 16

DOMINIQUE IS METICULOUSLY SEPARATING THE MOUND OF clean clothes on her bed, trying to get all of the shirts out before they wrinkle too badly. She hates ironing; besides from Betty homemaker, who doesn't hate ironing? She pulls out the last of the shirts and heads over to her closet, scavenging for empty hangers that hide between the tons of clothes that she has, but never wears. One day she'll clean out her closet. She starts hanging up her shirts when she hears a knock on the front door followed with it opening. She jumps a little, momentarily forgetting that she unlocked it for Jordan to come in. Dominique walks out of her room and down the hall.

"Hey, where are you?" Jordan asks from the entry way.

Dominique steps into the entry, "Right here," she smiles and gives Jordan a big hug. Jordan hugs her back with the same intensity, "Thank you."

Confused, she asks, "For what?"

"For being such a great friend. Helping me through the whole prom fiasco. Being my sparring partner, you know, stuff like that."

Jordan lets go of Dominique and steps back so that she can look her in the eyes, "Of course. You would have done the same for me. What brought those memories up?"

"I told Tracy about it."

"Oh, wow. Big step."

"Yeah, you could say that. Hey, come back with me to my room. I'm putting my laundry away."

"Alright. I want to see that locket, too."

"Yeah, right, it's crazy, isn't it?"

They walk into her room and Dominique walks over to the wooden box sitting on her dresser and pulls out the locket. She hands it to Jordan.

"It's beautiful – definitely an antique," she rubs her thumb against the design on the gold then opens it, "Oh my god, that is so you!"

"I know. I think my dad is trying to contact me…but why after nearly twenty-six years would he decide to do it now?"

"I don't know. You're mom has quite a few secrets about the whole paternal family thing."

"I know, and you won't believe what she said when I drove her home the other night."

"What?"

"She actually said she was going to talk to me about it all, that it was about time she did."

"Really? Was she drunk?" she laughs at the impossible thought.

"Actually, she was."

"Ah, that's uncharacteristic. Must be why she hasn't talked about them before."

"I knew it was a heavy topic for her, but I had no idea that it would later result in vomiting in the bushes. I haven't brought it up since that night. I wonder if she remembers telling me she would talk about it."

Dominique walks back over to the bed and continues putting her clothes away, clearing a spot for Jordan to sit. Jordan places the locket back in the box and checks her face in the mirror. She sees the silver cross hanging from the edge of the mirror and touches it.

"Why don't you have this on? You always wear this."

Dominique turns and looks at what she is referring to then goes back to folding, "I've been getting a rash from the cross. It's totally weird. The chain doesn't bother me, but the charm does."

"That is weird. Are they made of the same metal?"

"I thought so, but maybe the chain is white gold and the cross is silver, or vice versa. I don't know. I keep meaning to coat the cross with some clear nail polish so that it does not come into direct contact with my skin. I thought that might help."

"Yeah. I've done that with a couple of rings I reacted to and it works for a while. That is still strange."

"Allergies can change. I used to be allergic to olive oil, but I cook with it all the time now."

"Olive oil?"

"Yeah, I guess when I was a baby my grandma and mom took me to church to be Christened. The pastor must have used olive oil to anoint me or something. My head blistered."

"That had to be traumatic for your mom."

"Yeah."

Chapter 17

June, 1978

CLOUDS KEEP INTERRUPTING THE OTHERWISE BEAUTIFUL
sunny day. The planters in the courtyard of the Presbyterian church
are full of vibrant flowers planted by the women of the church.
Metal carts holding hot coffee and juice sit beside another cart
holding breakfast pastries, cut in half and neatly arranged by the
devout women of the church. Greeters help the parish get their
snacks before service starts, while others stand and catch up on the
gossip from the past week. Jade is sitting barefoot on the lawn
wearing a long spring dress, bottle feeding Dominique, who is now
six months old.

Betty walks over to her daughter and reaches down for
Dominique, "Here, I'll burp her while you put your shoes back on.
We need to go inside."

Jade stands up and brushes the back of her dress, removing the
few pieces of cut grass. She looks out across the parking lot,
hoping to see Shadow, but knowing that it was not possible to share

this with him. She picks up the diaper bag and follows her mom into the sanctuary. Betty greets everyone as they make their way to the front pews. She hands Dominique back to Jade once they sit down. Jade starts feeding her again while the pastor gets up in front of the congregation.

"Good morning," Pastor Miller greets his parish.

"Good morning," they respond in unison.

"And what a beautiful morning it is today. Today is a special Sunday. Not that every Sunday is not special, but this one is especially special because we all get to bare witness to a new member joining the family of God. Today is the Christening of Dominique McCloud. Would you three come up here?"

Betty and Jade stand up and walk up to the pulpit, next to the wooden baptismal. Pastor Miller extends his arms and Jade hands the baby to him.

"What a beautiful little girl," he holds her up so the congregation can see, "Wouldn't you all agree?"

Affirmation comes from the pews along with some 'ooos' and 'awes'. He cradles Dominique in one arm and lifts the lid off of the baptismal. He sets his Bible down on the edge of the baptismal and pulls the satin ribbon, opening the Bible to the appropriate passage.

"As it was declared in the first book of Peter, chapter three, verses eighteen through twenty-two, For Christ died for sins once for all, the righteous for the unrighteous, to bring you to God. He was put to death in the body, but made alive by the Spirit, through whom also he went and preached to the spirits in prison who disobeyed long ago when God waited patiently in the days of Noah while the ark was being built. In it only a few people, eight in all, were saved through water, and this water symbolizes baptism," he cups his hand in the water and lets it drip from his palm, "that now saves you also – not the removal of dirt from the body but the pledge of a good conscience towards God. It saves you by the resurrection of Jesus Christ, who has gone into heaven and is at God's right hand – with angels, authorities and powers in submission to him."

Pastor Miller closes the Bible and sets it aside. He cradles Dominique over the baptismal, cups some water in his free hand,

"In the name of the Father," he pours the water on top of her little head.

Dominique screams at the top of her lungs. Jade looks over at her innocent baby with worry in her eyes.

"I guess she doesn't like that," Pastor Miller tries to make light of the situation, "The Son," he pours more water over her head.

Dominique screams again, as if in excruciating pain. Jade snatches her from the pastor's arms and gently wipes her head off with a receiving blanket. Small blisters have started to develop on her tender head.

"What's in that water?" Jade asks, showing Dominique's head to her mother and the pastor.

"Oh, dear. It's just water," the Pastor states while sniffing the water.

The congregation starts to stir. Betty puts her hand in the water, then sniffs it herself.

"It doesn't have an odor. Maybe the oil is bad," she states referring to the olive oil the pastor sprinkled into the water earlier.

"I am so sorry," Pastor Miller states with great sincerity.

"It's ok, I'm just going to go. Mom, let's go," Jade walks down the steps and grabs the diaper bag on her way out of the church, not giving her mom a chance to argue.

Betty makes her way to the pew and picks up her purse. She picks up her pace to catch up with her daughter.

Jade is standing in the courtyard, trying to consol her crying baby.

Betty hurries over to her, "Come on, let's go to the bathroom and try to wash off the oil," she takes the diaper bag from her daughter and starts towards the bathroom.

Jade follows her while Betty rummages through the bag. She pulls out some baby wash before opening the door to the restroom. She holds the door open for Jade who hurries past her to the sink. Jade turns on the water, monitoring the temperature with her hand, Betty puts some soap on a washcloth. She puts the cloth under the water and suds it up then gently places it on the baby's head. Almost immediately, Dominique stops crying. The compress cools her blistering head, alleviating the pain. After a few seconds, Betty removes the washcloth and inspects her head.

"She must be allergic to olive oil," she states, shaking her head.

Betty rinses out the cloth and wipes the soap from her head; the blisters start to fade away.

"Oh, thank God," Betty states, "They're going away."

Jade holds her baby close to her, kissing her forehead, "I am so sorry, baby girl. I am so sorry. We'll never do that again."

Dominique starts to coo and nestles her head on Jade's breasts. Jade holds her tight while Betty puts everything away.

"Let's go home," Jade says more to Dominique than to Betty.

* * *

After her rough Christening experience, Dominique is sleeping soundly in her crib. Her mobile, playing *Twinkle, Twinkle Little Star*, is starting to wind down while Jade sits on her bed, holding an old rotary phone on her lap, contemplating whether or not to make the inevitable phone call. She picks up the receiver and starts dialing the number.

"Hello?" a woman's voice answers.

"Hello. Uh, may I speak to Shadow?"

"May I ask who is calling?"

"Jade," she responds, trying to control her trembling voice.

"One moment, please."

Jade can hear the phone being set down on a table and the sound of heals clicking across the stone floor. Jade anxiously sits there contemplating hanging up the phone, but reminds herself that she has already told them who she was.

"Hello," Shadow states.

"Hi," Jade responds.

"Is everything ok?"

"Um, well, I'm not sure. Are you allergic to olive oil?"

"Weird and random."

"Well, you see, we went to the church today to have Dominique Christened and when the Pastor poured the water over her head it started to blister. I thought it might be the olive oil he sprinkled in the water."

"Oh, I see. No, I'm not allergic. She could have had a reaction to the water."

"What do you mean? I give her baths all the time. She's never had this reaction before," she states, defensively.

"You don't usually bless the bath water, do you?"

"No."

"That was probably the problem."

"What do you mean?"

"Well, I'm not exactly Christian, nor will I ever be."

"Did you know this would happen?" she asks, standing up, frustrated.

"No. How would I? I've never come across this. This was not exactly an issue in my family. I would not allow anything to harm her!" he responds, defensively.

"What does this mean? She can't be a Christian?" she states, trying to calm down.

"I suppose she could be. You have just had her indoctrinated into a religion at an age where she is unable to make the decision. It's like forcing her to be a Christian against her will. She may decide that she wants to chose that path, though it may be more difficult when she comes of age," he responds.

"Oh, I can't deal with this right now!" she hangs up the phone and plops back down on her bed.

* * *

Jade steps out of the steamy shower and wraps herself with a towel. She walks over to the mirror and rests her palms on the sink. Dangling her head over the basin, she sighs deeply then takes the hand towel and wipes the condensation from the mirror. She stares intently at herself, examining the dark circles under her eyes and the crows feet that are starting to prematurely develop on her seventeen year old face. She pulls open the medicine cabinet and takes out some Oil of Olay and rubs it on her premature wrinkles in hopes of stopping them before they take over her face. She closes the mirror and walks out of the bathroom and heads down the hall to the room she shares with her daughter. Gently, she opens the cracked door and enters the night light illuminated room and walks over to the crib. Dominique is fast asleep, suckling on her bottom lip. Jade goes over to her dresser and takes out a burgundy sweat suit and gets dressed. She pulls her hair back into a bun and leaves the room. The warm smell of chicken enchiladas greets her as she walks down the hall towards the kitchen. Betty is setting the homemade meal out on the table between the two place settings when Jade walks in.

"It smells great, Mom," Jade states, taking in the scent.

"Your favorite. Mexican," she replies while filling the glasses with southern style sweet tea.

Jade sits down at the table and takes a drink of the sweet amber liquid. Betty sits down opposite of Jade and places her napkin in her lap. She takes the spatula and cuts out two enchiladas. Jade sticks her plate out so Betty can place the food on it.

"Did you actually cook this?"

"Yes, I sent Cynthia home early. Her little one is sick."

"Thank you so much, Mom."

"You are welcome," she responds while serving herself.

Jade takes her fork and slices off a piece, blowing on it before taking a bite.

"How was your shower?"

"Good, just what I needed. Thank you for keeping an eye on her."

"No problem. I was happy to," Betty hesitates a moment, "You had a phone call while you were in the shower."

"Oh, who called?"

"Andreas."

Jade puts her fork back down on her plate and wipes her mouth, "Really? What did he want?"

"He wanted to see you tonight."

"What did you tell him?"

"I told him that I would pass on the message."

Jade raises her eyebrow, "You did?"

"Well, honey, it's up to you. You are an adult now. You have a child, for crying out loud. You can make the decision to see him. Like it or not, and I do not like it at all, he is the father of your child. He does have the right to see her."

"Is that what he asked? To see Dominique?"

"No, but I assume that's why he wants to see you. To arrange a time to see his daughter," she shutters at the thought of him being her granddaughter's father.

"Oh."

Jade continues eating, as the wheels turn in her head.

"That's it? 'Oh'?"

"Yeah, I guess. I don't know what to say, Mom. You were right. I should have stayed away from him. You knew he was bad news and I wouldn't listen to you. Is that what you want to hear?" she asks as the temperature rises in her face.

"I don't think an 'I told you so' is necessary. I know you have your regrets. I have my regrets for you. I do not, however, regret Dominique being born. Not for one second," she pulls her napkin from her lap and wipes her mouth.

"I don't either. I love my little girl," she takes a breath, "I'll see him. I'll see what he wants."

"And I will support you."

"Thank you, Mom," she scoots away from the table and takes her plate over to the sink, "Will you listen for Nickie while I'm gone?"

"Of course."

"Thank you."

Jade rinses her plate off and dumps the iced tea down the sink. She wonders what he wants, the day has been devastating enough and she doesn't think she can take any more bad news. She dries her hands then hangs the towel back on the rack. Picking up her keys, she walks out to her car and reaches for the door handle. Shadow walks up beside her.

"Hey."

Jade jumps around and faces Shadow. She smacks him on the arm, "You scared the crap out of me!"

"Sorry about that. I just thought you might be willing to see me so I came over."

"Ok, what do you want?"

"Want to walk?"

"Sure," Jade puts her keys in her pocket.

Shadow nervously runs his fingers through his hair, "Other than the unpleasant incident at the church, how's Dominique doing?"

"She's great. The best baby in the world. Hardly cries and is already sleeping through the night. She's just so precious," Jade states proudly.

"That's wonderful. I'm glad things are going ok."

"My mom is a great help."

Shadow pulls a checkbook out of his pocket and hands it to Jade, "Here, this is for you."

Jade gives him a confused look, "What's this?"

"Just open it to the first check."

Jade opens up the check book. The top of the check has Jade's name on it.

"Before you object, it is my duty to take care of my child and with that the mother of my child. I want you to be taken care of and not feel as if you must work to take care of yourself. I want your only worry to be taking care of Dominique."

"I don't know…" Jade looks at the checks, unsure of what her obligations might entail.

"This is your account. I opened it in your name this morning. There's enough money for you to do whatever you want to do. Buy a house, buy a car, groceries, diapers, whatever you want. You never need to worry about being low on funds. There will always be money in this account."

Jade hesitates then stops herself, "This is nice of you, but what do you want?"

"I want you to be able to take care of yourself. No strings attached. It's my duty to do this."

"Thank you."

"No need to thank me. I should have set this up months ago."

Jade puts the checkbook in her back pocket. Lightning flashes followed by the rumble of thunder rolling through the night sky. Clouds start to come in bringing sprinkles along with it.

"I also want you to know that I've come up with a business plan."

"A business plan? For what? You don't need to work."

"No, but I need to eat and it's getting harder to get what we need to survive without drawing attention to ourselves. Besides, I was never a huge fan of the traditional method."

Jade's stomach curdles at the thought of drinking blood, "Yeah, well, me neither."

"So, I'm going to open a blood bank. We're going to call the corporation New Blood. This way people are donating their blood. Some of it will go to hospitals and other emergencies, the rest will go to the vampire community."

"Still gross, but it sounds like a better method to me."

"I thought you would say that. I also hoped it would help you to not look at me with repulsion."

Jade stops walking and turns to Shadow, "I've never been repulsed by you. I love you," she tries to look in his eyes, but tears start welling up. She turns away from him to hide her face and starts walking again, "I'm just afraid of you."

"You don't need to be afraid of me, Jade. I would never do anything to hurt you," he picks up his pace to catch up with her.

"Ok, maybe you won't. But what about Sabin? He's just waiting for the chance to change me. I have nightmares about it."

The wind screams through the trees as the rain starts to pelt down on top of them.

"Sabin will not do anything to you. He knows how I feel about it and he will not do something that I feel adamant about."

"If you say so. I need to go in and feed Dominique."

"Ok."

"When are you going to start this blood bank?"

"I have a meeting to talk with the elders tomorrow. If all goes well, I should be up and running in a month."

Jade nods her head in understanding, "Well, I hope it works out."

"Thank you."

Jade walks up the sidewalk to her front door, "Goodnight."

"Goodnight."

Jade walks into the house and turns to watch Shadow leave, but he is already gone.

Chapter 18

June, 1978

THE ELDERS HAVE ARRIVED AND ARE TALKING AMONGST themselves at the large oval shaped conference table sitting in the center of a large room, obviously part of Sabin and Shadow's home. Behind heavy dark curtains are metal plates drawn closed as to not allow a smidgen of sunlight into the room. A low hanging chandelier softly lights the room and accentuates the table centerpiece – a large ornate stainless steel coffee style carafe. One of the elders loosens his tie while others begin to fidget.

"I apologize for my brother's tardiness. I am sure he is just finishing up the final touches of his presentation. Meanwhile, can I get anyone something to drink?" Sabin stands up from the head of the table and starts towards a drink cart.

"Yeah, a young boy," Sedrick states, smugly.

They all laugh at his joke.

Sabin smirks, "We will dine later."

Shadow walks into the room with a manila folder under his arm, "I apologize for being late, but I assure you it will be worth your time."

"It better be," Aaron scoffs.

"Yeah, this better be good. I was supposed to be in Paris this afternoon," Matilda states with a hint of annoyance in her voice.

Shadow nods at Sabin, "Could you hit the lights?"

Shadow places his folder down on the table and picks up a metal rod with a hook at the end, lifts it up to the handle attached to the projection screen and pulls it down. He removes the cap from the slide projector that is already on and ready to go. Picking up the remote to the slide machine, he steps to the side to start his presentation.

"Now, ladies and gentleman, I would like to propose a method of obtaining nourishment without the anxiety of being caught. As you can see here, I have made a chart of the ease of the hunt in years past versus the difficulty we now have."

Shadow uses a pointer stick to highlight some figures from the turn of the century to the present. He flips through a few more slides showing photos.

"Remember Vincent, Angelo, Leticia?"

He continues flipping through photos of dead vampires.

Some of the elders turn their heads, not wanting to remember the horrific deaths of their brothers and sisters.

"How could we not? It's getting harder to hunt, we all know this, so what is your proposal? Farming humans?"

"I have an idea that will make humans willingly give us their blood."

The elders roll their eyes, not believing his proposal.

"Are you wasting our time?" Matilda sneers.

Shadow ignores the question, "Not only will they give us their blood for free, but we will make a profit from this venture. I propose that we open blood banks. A legitimate business, that will be called New Blood, Incorporated. We can hire werewolves to manage the businesses during the day. Hell, we can even hire humans to draw the blood for us. We collect the blood from local offices and send the blood to a lab, where the blood is refined and tested."

"Stale blood? You want us to drink stale, cold blood?" Sedrick asks, unbelieving.

"No, I do not," Sabin walks over to the carafe and takes a wine glass. He flips the nozzle and blood trickles into the glass. Every vampire in the room reacts to the scent of the blood. He hands it to Sedrick, "Try this."

The elder crinkles up his nose, "Disgusting, no."

"You won't be disappointed."

He takes the glass of warm blood and tentatively takes a sip. Then he downs the rest, "Ok, where's the human?" He looks under the table to see if someone is under it hooked to an IV.

"Oxygenated warmed blood is the answer to our problems. Collecting blood is not enough. After sitting for a while it's stale and gross. We can oxygenate it and warm it to body temperature. It tastes like it came straight from a live vein. When, in fact, the blood is a month old."

"It doesn't taste a month old," he stands up and takes the empty glass in front of Matilda and pours a glass for her, "Drink."

They all eagerly go for their glasses and pour blood into them. They drink until they are full.

"What do you need from us?"

"Your approval and support. I need you all to base these blood banks in your cities, financially back them and the laboratory, until we get going, then it will support itself. You will get your money back."

"Who cares about getting our money back, this will help grow our population!" Sedrick states full of enthusiasm.

Shadow nods at Sabin, who turns on the lights, "I have business plans prepared for each of you. All you need to do is follow it verbatim and you are set. It also explains how we will actually donate some of the blood to hospitals and such as to appear legitimate."

"What ever we need to do for this to be a success. Good job, my boy, good job," Aaron raises his glass, "To New Blood, Inc!"

* * *

The clouds have cleared the once stormy sky and have allowed the sun to seep through. Jade's VW bug is parked outside a medium sized two story French Tudor home with a 'for sale' sign in the front yard. The front yard is nicely landscaped with topiaries planted on either side of the entry way and gardenia bushes lined up in front of the house.

Jade, holding Dominique, and her mother are standing in the entry way, watching the realtor unlock the door. They walk into the foyer, and are greeted with high ceilings and hardwood floors. Jade takes in the scent of the house. The airiness and space makes her smile.

"And this is it," Frank states as he walks in front of them, turning around to face them, "This is the one I thought you would find perfect."

"Ahh, so far so good," Jade states, happily.

"Good, then follow me."

Frank guides them through the house and into a comfortably large living room with a fireplace. Betty takes Dominique from Jade while she walks over to the oversized windows. Jade looks up at the texture in the ceiling and, trance like, walks out of the room and explores the rest of the house. As she walks through the house it starts to feel like a home to her. She can see her future furniture in place and imagine the smell of the meals that she will prepare for herself and her daughter. She makes her way into the backyard that is beautifully landscaped with an incredible garden that surrounds a waterfall that flows into a Koi pond. She walks over to a handcrafted bench that rests in front of the pond and sits down. Betty walks into the back yard and is taken aback by the beauty.

"Wow, this is amazing. It's like walking into another world."

"I love it, Mom. It's so peaceful. I could paint all day here."

Betty walks over to the bench and sits down. Dominique reaches for her momma; Jade takes her.

"What do you think, honey? Do you like it here? Plenty of room to play and run."

Dominique smiles at Jade and coos at her.

"Well, Dominique likes it," Betty smiles at them, "You know, you don't have to move out. You don't have to take his money. It's not like we can't make do."

"I'm not taking his money. He's offering it to help raise his daughter, as he should. He might not need to give so much, but I appreciate it. I would really like my own home. It's not like I'm going to be frivolous with it."

"I know. I'm sure this is for the best."

Frank walks into the back yard, "So?"

"I'll take it."

"Great, I'll get the paperwork going."

* * *

Several weeks later, Jade and Dominique have moved into their new home. Jade has carefully picked out drapes, furniture and other decorations to make the house feel warm and welcoming. Shadow has been on her mind throughout the entire experience. Every time she pulled out the checkbook to pay for something or withdrew cash from the bank, she thought of him, the good times they had together. It wasn't until she learned of her pregnancy that their life together became difficult. She wants so badly for them to work out, but is it possible? Can she be who she is, raise Dominique the way she wants her raised, and have him be a father to her?

Dominique is peacefully sleeping in a basinet Jade has placed in the living room so she can keep her close to her during nap time. Jade is sitting in front of a canvas that she has set up in front of one of the large windows and is painting. She sits back for a moment, looking at her creation, then looks over at Dominique, her other creation; Shadow's creation as well. She puts her paint brush down on her easel and walks over to the phone. She sits down in the plush chair next to the phone table and picks up the receiver. She takes a deep breath, then dials. The phone rings several times, Jade almost gives up.

"Hello?" a man's voice answers the phone.

Jade, surprised, "I think I have the wrong number," she starts to hang up the phone.

"Jade, is that you?"

Jade puts the phone back to her ear, "Yes, who is this?"

"It's Shadow."

"Oh, I expected the maid to answer."

"Oh, yeah, well, she's a little busy with Sabin right now."

"Oh."

"So, is everything ok?"

"Oh, yeah, everything is fine. I, uh, just thought that I would invite you over for dinner. I want you to see the house you bought."

"Oh," Shadow's tone changes from one of concern to excitement, "I would love to. When?"

"Tonight? Seven o'clock?"

"Yeah, that would be wonderful."

"I thought I would barbeque. Rare, right? Baked potatoes, salad."

"Sounds perfect. I'll bring some wine."

Jade smiles; her heart flutters with excitement, "Ok, well, I'll see you at seven."

"I'll be there," he hangs up the phone.

Jade hangs up the phone and sits motionless for a moment. She can hardly believe that she had the courage to invite him over. She can hardly believe that she was crazy enough to invite him over. The smile she had slowly fades from her face. What if Sabin tries something? What if he thinks of this as going against their agreement? She takes in a deep breath and walks over to her daughter. Seeing that she is still sleeping peacefully she walks into the kitchen and opens her refrigerator. She picks up a pad of paper and a pen from the counter and starts making a list of everything she needs to get at the grocery store. Shadow won't let Sabin do anything to her. If this relationship is reconcilable, if it is possible for her to stay who she is, not change into one of them, and have Shadow in their lives, that's what she wants. She wants Dominique to have a relationship with her father. She decides it's better to try and build a relationship with Shadow now and have it fail while

Dominique is too young to remember than to wait until she is older. Jade smiles as she closes the refrigerator. Yes, this is the best way to go.

* * *

Jade's living room is warmly lit with candles placed throughout the room. Flames flicker in front of the mirror hanging over the fireplace, giving the illusion of more light than there really is. The foyer light is dim, but bright enough to see where she is going. Baked potatoes and a hint of the spice scented candles fill the entire house giving it the warm "welcome home" scent that was usually absent in the McCloud home of Jade's youth.

In the kitchen, Dominique is sitting in her high chair, apple sauce all over her face, smiling from ear to ear. Jade takes a wet washcloth and wipes her face.

"You like this don't you?"

Dominique giggles at her mom, as if she's trying to get as messy as possible before their house guest comes to dinner. Jade puts the lid back on the glass Gerber baby food jar and puts it in the refrigerator. She picks up Dominique and puts her on her hip.

"Ok, Nickie, let's check on those steaks."

She walks to the other side of the kitchen and opens the back door, grabbing a cookie sheet and a serving fork on her way out the door. She sets the cookie sheet down on the patio table next to the grill and removes the lid, hooking it on the side of the briquette grill. She sticks the fork in one of the steaks, seared brown on both sides, it still bleeds when the fork is removed.

"Well, Daddy's is done."

She sticks the fork back in the steak and takes it off the grill, placing it on the cookie sheet. She presses her steak with the fork, checking it's density. She sticks the fork in it and pulls it out, no blood.

"Perfect," she says as she removes her steak from the fire.

She places the fork on top of the steaks and takes them into the house just as the doorbell rings. Her stomach sinks and her heart starts to flutter. She looks at Dominique and kisses her on the forehead, "Here we go."

She walks through the kitchen into the foyer, takes a deep breath and opens the door. Shadow is standing there, clean shaven and wearing a tight white t-shirt, holding a bouquet of fresh wild flowers and a bottle of wine.

"Hi," Jades smiles, "Come in."

Shadow walks in the house and kisses Jade on the cheek, "Thank you for inviting me."

Jade takes in his cologne, and melts inside from the irresistible scent and the feeling of his lips on her cheek. She closes the door, trying to get her head together, she lets out a heavy breath.

"Trade you?" Shadow hands over the flowers and wine and motions to Dominique.

"Oh, yeah, sure," she hands Dominique to Shadow and takes the flowers and wine.

Shadow holds Dominique up to his face and looks at every detail, "She's beautiful."

"Well, I guess we make pretty babies."

Shadow smiles, "I guess we do," he kisses his daughter on the cheek then cradles her.

"Well, let's go to the kitchen so I can put these in some water."

Shadow follows her in the kitchen, looking around at what he can see of the house, "I like the house. It's what I expected you to get."

"Is it?" Jade responds pulling a vase out of a cupboard.

"Yes, just enough. You know, not too flashy, not too modern, very comfortable."

"Thank you. We love it," she cuts the ends off the flowers and puts them in the vase. She fills the vase with water then pulls a bottle of bleach out from under the sink. Pouring a capful of bleach, she pours it in the water.

"Bleach?"

"Oh, yeah, a secret my mom taught me. A little bleach keeps them fresher longer; too much and they die."

"Good to know."

She takes the flowers and wine and walks into the dining room. She puts the flowers in the center of the table and places the wine near the head of the table. Place settings for two are already set up, one at the head of the table and one next to it. She walks back into the kitchen and opens the oven. After grabbing an oven mitt, she pulls out the two baked potatoes and sticks a knife in one of them. It pulls out smoothly.

"Ok, everything is done. You want to pull her high chair into the dining room while I get dinner on the table?"

"Sure, no problem."

Jade watches Shadow as he puts Dominique on his hip and lifts the high chair with his free hand and takes it into the dining room. Her heart starts to flutter again. How magnificent it would be to have help raising Dominique. She loves her daughter to death, but help is a great thing, especially if the help is Shadow. She tries to wipe the hope from her mind as she takes the food to the table.

"Do you have a bib for her?"

"Oh, no, she's already eaten. Applesauce. I'm going to give her breast milk after we eat and put her down."

He puts Dominique down in the high chair that he has placed between the two chairs.

"Where do you want me to sit?"

"Go ahead and sit at the head. It's easier if she is on my right."

He takes a seat while Jade puts the last of the food on the table. She walks over to her chair and sits down.

"That one's yours," she says pointing to the rare steak.

He picks up the serving fork and picks up her steak, motioning for Jade to hand him her plate.

She picks up her plate and holds it for him, "Thank you."

"Thank you for cooking and for inviting me over."

Jade smiles as she sets her plate down. She picks up a baked potato and puts it on her plate. She cuts it open, steam rises up from it. She takes the butter knife and cuts off a hunk of butter and lathers her potato. Shadow takes the salad tongs and puts some salad on his plate.

"Is this Italian dressing?"

"Yes, another one of my mom's secrets," she smiles at him, "I am so glad that you are here."

Dominique starts to fuss a little at the lack of attention her parents are giving her. Jade picks up her spoon and hands it to her.

"Sorry, little one."

Dominique takes the spoon from her, and happily starts banging the metal tray with it.

"I see she wants to be a musician," Shadow says, elevating his voice over the rhythm.

"Yes, an all girl rock band, of course."

"Of course."

Shadow cuts into his steak, his pupils dilate in anticipation. He takes the first bite and chews it slowly, letting the blood run down his throat.

"This tastes fantastic. I like the seasoning."

"I'm sure you do."

The sinking feeling she once had starts to fade away as she remembers how he usually gets his nutrition. Her smile starts to disappear.

"What just happened?"

"Oh, nothing," she takes a bite of her potato.

"How about some wine?" Shadow grabs the bottle of wine and the corkscrew.

"Sure, just a little though."

He uncorks the bottle and pours them both a glass of wine, "Bordeaux, from my collection. I remember that you like the sweet wines best."

"Thank you," she takes a sip of the sweet, dark liquid, "Because of you I am such a wine snob. All of my friends, well the ones who sneak wine from their parents bar, drink cheap table wines."

Shadow laughs, "There's nothing wrong with experiencing the best and accepting nothing less than. This is definitely not 'cheap' wine," he picks up the bottle and looks at the label, "It's fifty years old."

"Amazing," she takes another sip.

"You know, I do absorb nutrition from food, you know, like this," he unfolds his hand moves it over his plate.

"Ok."

"I saw the look on your face when I said I liked the flavor of the meat. I do like the flavor. I need blood more than the rest of this, but I can survive on this. I just have to eat rare red meat. Dominique will have to as she grows up as well."

Jade looks over at her daughter who is now pushing the spoon around her tray. She has a sudden feeling of fear as she thinks about what it means to raise her daughter. The daughter of Shadow. A vampire. A blood sucking vampire.

"Does that mean that she is not getting enough nutrition now? It's not like I can give her beef."

"She's fine as long as she still gets breast milk. As soon as she doesn't, you need to feed her food high in iron."

Jade starts to relax a little, "So, vitamins with iron in them is enough?"

"It's a start. Supplement that with almonds, broccoli, kidney beans, prunes. There are several other foods that contain iron like tuna, liver, and especially beef. As she grows older she will start to crave the flavor of blood. She'll want rare meat more than the other foods."

"Oh," Jade sets her fork down across her plate, discouraged as she learns that her baby will crave blood.

"It doesn't mean she's going to crave killing," he puts his fork down and places his hand on hers, "I don't. In fact, I would rather eat steak, or take the blood from an animal than from a human."

"Can we stop this conversation now? I don't want to think about my little girl…doing that."

Jade stands up and picks up Dominique, "I need to go feed her now."

"I'm sorry, Jade, but I thought you would want to know what her special needs will be."

"No, I do need to know this. It's just hard to process, is all. I'll be back down in about a half hour. You can finish eating, if you want."

"Yeah, I'll finish eating."

"Ok."

Jade heads out of the dining room and starts up the stairs. Their conversation runs through her head like a broken record. Her little girl is not all human. She is part monster. Part Shadow, the man she once loved. The man she still loves.

She looks down at Dominique as she walks into the master bedroom, "Make sure you know everything about the man you have sex with before you have sex with him."

Dominique blinks her tired eyes at her mom and rests her head against her chest. Jade sits down in the rocker recliner that sits in front of her bedroom window. She unbuttons her shirt and unhooks her bra. Dominique latches on and starts suckling as Jade sits back and starts rocking. She rubs her palm across Dominique's soft head and watches as her eyes grow heavier and heavier. Tears well up in her eyes as she looks at her sweet innocent baby. She had no choice in her making. She is here out of passion, a passion that she could not control and now she has to walk the earth as this thing – half mortal.

"But she is still my little girl, my beautiful daughter. I will always protect you and will never treat you any different."

She pulls Dominique, who is sleeping peacefully, away from her breast and holds her tight against her and starts patting her back, and rocking. Dominique awakens momentarily then quickly drifts back to sleep. Jade's ears perk up as she hears the sound of footsteps coming up the stairs. Shadow walks to the doorway. Jade stands up and puts Dominique into her crib. She covers her up halfway with a blanket then winds the mobile attached to the crib. Shadow walks over and looks down at the baby.

"She's so peaceful."

"Yes, she really is."

Jade walks to the doorway then turns around when she realizes Shadow isn't behind her. She stands for a moment, watching him looking at his daughter. Her feelings of love for him well up in her body once again. She tries to shake off the feeling, but is unsuccessful. Shadow looks over at her, melting her heart, then walks over to her. He takes her hand and guides her downstairs to the living room. He walks her over to the couch and they sit down.

"You made a fire."

"Yeah, I thought it was chilly enough. Is that ok?"

"Yeah, it's nice."

He picks up the bottle of wine that he brought in from the dinner table and pours them each a glass. He hands one to Jade.

"Thank you," she takes a sip.

Shadow takes a drink, "Thank you, again, for dinner. I'm sorry that it entailed an unpleasant moment for you."

Jade nods, "Things I need to know, I guess," she takes another drink then sets her glass on the table, "How was your proposal?"

"My proposal?"

"With the elders."

"Oh, yeah, excellent. They loved the idea. I hope to have business up and running in the next six months."

"Good, I'm happy for you."

"Be happy for us."

"Us?"

"Well, this venture will potentially produce a lot of money, which will go to you and Dominique as well."

"Well, about that."

"About what?"

"The money. I really do appreciate the money and it has really helped get me going, but I plan on paying you back for the house. Anything not specifically for Nickie, I will pay you back for."

"There's no need for that. I intended on providing for you and for Dominique."

"I just don't feel right about it. I don't want to owe you anything."

"You don't owe me anything. Providing for Dominique means providing for you. I will be completely insulted if you don't use the money I have given you."

Jade thinks about what he said for a moment. He looks as if he is hurt by the conversation to begin with.

"Ok, I will accept the money."

"Good," he finishes off his wine and sets the glass on the table. He props himself against the arm of the couch and puts his right arm out against the back of the couch, inviting Jade to lean against him.

Jade hesitantly scoots closer to him and lies against him, placing her head on his chest. She closes her eyes as her body sinks into his body, a feeling so familiar and comforting to her. She takes her arm and slides it across his firm abs. It's been several months since she has felt his warmth; she almost forgot what it felt like. Almost. Slowly, she grips around his waist and snuggles in closer, scooting her head closer to his heart. She listens to the rhythmic beat of his pulse. He can't be immortal. Vampires hearts don't beat, right? They surely can't be warm. They can't feel this good, can they?

Shadow kisses the top of her head and tenderly rubs her arm with his soft hand. He squeezes her gently.

"I just…"

"What, babe?"

She turns her body so that her back is on his lap, so she can look him in the face. She reaches up and touches his face. Trying to find the words, she opens her mouth, but decides against it. Words cannot describe the explosion that is going on inside her mind and body. She sits up and kisses him. Passion runs through her veins as she satisfies what she has wanted to do all evening. He pulls her closer to him and picks her up, cradling her in his arms as if she weighed as much as their baby daughter. She wraps her arms around his neck as he stands up and starts to carry her upstairs to the master bedroom. She kisses, then tenderly bites his neck. He pauses on the stairs, momentarily, having to catch his balance. The feeling of her teeth against his skin made his knees buckle. Quietly, as to not wake Dominique, Shadow walks into the room and lies Jade down on the bed. She pulls the covers down while he pulls off his t-shirt and throws it to the side. She lies down on the bed; he lies on top of her and kisses her some more. Goosebumps form on her delicate skin. He unbuttons her shirt, lifts her up, letting it fall off her body. Jade lies back on the bed and looks up at him. Desire and fear fill her eyes. Flashes of Sabin's words race through her mind. She tries to wipe them away.

I told you, brother, you should have taken her when you had a chance. Now it's too risky for the baby. You'll have to wait until she delivers.

Shadow kisses her neck as he slides his hand over her breast, cupping it softly. Gently, he starts to bite down on her neck. Jade jumps and pushes him away from her. He quickly sits up beside her. She puts her hand on her neck and wipes it, checking it for blood. A small drop appears on her hand. Her eyes widen in terror as she gets out of bed and rushes into the master bathroom. She flips on the light and looks in the mirror. A small hole, the size of a pinprick leaks some blood from its opening. Shadow walks in behind her.

"I'm sorry. I thought you were giving me a hint when you bit my neck on the stairway."

"I don't want to change," she replies weakly as she wipes the blood from her neck.

"What do you want?"

She turns around to face him, "I want us to be a family. I want to stay mortal, finish growing up. Experience what it's like to grow old."

"And die," he replies vehemently.

"Yes, one day."

"I cannot be here and watch your flesh grow old. Knowing that you will die one day while I will continue living...I can't do that. We can never be if this is what you want."

Jade's heart sinks. She steps closer to him and looks him in the eye, "Then we can't be."

As soon as the words leave her lips she crumbles inside. Her heart torn in two.

"Very well. You know where I am if you change your mind."

Jade looks down at the floor, trying not to cry. She looks up to face him, but he is gone. She walks out of the bathroom and looks down at her daughter, sleeping peacefully.

"Oh, baby, I hope I'm doing the right thing."

Chapter 19

DUSK IS STARTING TO SETTLE IN ON THIS HALLOWEEN NIGHT. Porch lights are starting to come on, blow up lawn ornaments imitating the monsters that haunt dreams are inflating while creepy music flows through neighborhoods. Some houses, more than others, prepare for this celebration of the dead, trying to outdo one another.

Dominique is standing in a black corset and matching lacy panties in front of the mirror in her bathroom curling her dark hair into long ringlets, trying to reproduce the hairdo of her ancestor in the locket. Hanging on a wooden hanger from the molding in the front of her closet is a Victorian style dress that she made, finding a pattern that was the closest to what little she could see in the picture. She twists her hair up and starts pinning it into the proper style for the time period. Once satisfied with her recreation, she starts to apply makeup, though unnecessary with her flawless complexion; she wants to get into the character of who she can only assume to be her great-grandmother. She looks over at the porcelain fangs she had made especially to fit her teeth and picks them up. They weren't cheap, but now that she pops in the retainer that holds the teeth into her mouth, she decides that they were well worth the investment. She runs her tongue across the points and smiles at how realistic they feel.

She walks into the bedroom and slips on the dress, zipping it up and then walks in front of the full length mirror.

Perfect, she thinks to herself. She looks over at the wood box on her dresser, *Almost perfect*.

She opens the box and puts on the locket.

"Nickie?"

She leaves her room and walks into the living room where Tracy has just settled herself.

"Wow, you look amazing," Tracy comments, taking her in.

Dominique smiles, flashing her fangs, "You look pretty amazing yourself."

Tracy walks over in her dominatrix leather outfit with a twist. Her face has been painted with dark, seductive makeup with lines drawn down the sides of her chin to look like a ventriloquists dummies mouth. A black top hat setting slightly towards the right of her head instead of straight on completes the ensemble. She motions for Dominique to turn around; she does, and then looks back at her face, focusing on the fangs.

"Oh my god! Those look incredibly real."

Dominique smiles, "They *feel* incredibly real," she states suggestively.

"Oh, really?"

"Yeah, want to feel?"

"You have to ask?" Tracy stands closer, taking Dominique by the waist and kisses her, running her tongue over the porcelain, "Wow," her body shivers at the several thoughts that start running through her mind; all of them good.

"Wow?" she smiles again.

"Yeah, I find them unbelievably seductive," she kisses her again.

Dominique gently pulls back, "We will never make it to the party at this rate."

"You're right, we should get going. But, we have to pick up where we left off later."

"Maybe," she teases.

"Maybe?"

"Yeah, maybe," she heads towards the front door, "Are you driving?"

"Yeah, I'll drive."

"Good, cause I don't want to leave my car up there if some hot chick decides to take me home."

"You are horrible," she smiles as Dominique opens the front door, grabbing her keys as she does.

"I figured you would be that hot chick."

"Ok, well in that case, let's go."

* * *

Tracy pulls her Jeep up the long gravel driveway that leads to the DeFleurs' castle. Event lights are crisscrossing through the sky, making sure everyone knows that there is something big going on at the DeFleur castle this night. People are posted along the way, directing traffic towards the valet parking that conveniently allows the guests to get out of their cars right in front of the house rather than trying to walk through the expansive property in their well put together costumes. Tracy pulls up to the valet and both doors are opened by men dressed in tuxes complete with cummerbunds and matching bowties. The man who opened Tracy's door hands her a ticket and speedily jumps in the Jeep and heads off to park it. Tracy walks over to Dominique, invitation in hand, and extends her elbow to escort her to the front door. Dominique puts her arm through Tracy's as they head down the walkway. The door opens, releasing the loud noises of a party that has been well on its way for a while. The hostess, dressed in a skimpy Goth dress complete with authentic fangs of her own, extends her hand for the invitation. Tracy hands it to her as she gives them both the once over. She hesitates at Dominique and looks at her more closely and smiles; Dominique smiles back, flashing her fangs.

"Those fangs look very natural on you," the hostess comments.

"Thanks. So do yours," she responds, raising her voice over the loud music.

The hostess nods and motions for them to enter the party. Tracy and Dominique walk into the massive room and take in the lengths that have been taken to create this atmosphere. The room holds a regal medieval feel to it; fancy goblets are being carried on silver platters by very attractive wait service staff, who are dressed like staff would be dressed at an upscale restaurant with a minor difference. They have added to their dress vampire fangs or face make-up so they look like werewolves.

The hostess lifts her right arm that is covered by the black fabric of her dress which conceals a mic right under the sleeve, "The Princess is here," she states with excitement. She looks up towards the balcony where Sabin and Shadow DeFleur sit regally in their high backed velvet lined chairs, observing as their guests come in. They nod down at the her, acknowledging that they heard her.

Sabin lifts his arm and speaks into his concealed mic, "Seth, they are here. Make sure they are comfortable."

"Yes, sir."

Shadow stands up and leans against the balcony and stares intently down at Dominique, taking her in, "She looks just like mother."

"Yes, I know."

"You never told me that the resemblance was so uncanny."

"I wanted you to see it for yourself, Brother."

"And that with her. That's her girl?"

"Yes, and a possible barrier for us to overcome."

Shadow turns around and looks at his brother, "You don't know that yet. Don't do anything irrational that will push her away before we get the chance to explain everything to her."

Sabin dramatically puts his hand up to his heart and gasps, "Would I do that?"

"Yes, you would, and please don't," he frowns at Sabin, "So far my method has worked, let's keep working my plan."

162

"As you wish," he states flippantly then stands up next to his brother, "well, I am going to go mingle. See if I can't find myself a dance partner."

"Right. Be careful, we don't need bodies lying around this early in the night."

"Tsk, tsk, little brother, tsk, tsk."

Sabin saunters off the balcony and down the stairs. His movement is not missed by anyone, men and women find themselves incredibly attracted to him. He joyously acknowledges his guests as he makes his way down to the main ballroom floor. All of them are eager to catch a glance or possibly touch him as he passes by. He scans the ballroom for a possible victim and then signals the waiter, who swiftly brings him over a goblet of dark red wine. He takes a long drink then licks his lips, placing the half empty glass back down on the tray and dismissing the waiter who obediently leaves. He looks over at Becky and Jill, the most recent additions to the family.

Come, he commands with his ability to speak telepathically.

The women look over towards Sabin and swiftly walk over to him.

"Yes, Master?" Becky greets.

"They are here. You know what you need to do."

Sabin sends them an image of where Dominique and Tracy are standing and they turn simultaneously and see them standing in the exact spot in Sabin's mind. They look back at Sabin and nod in understanding, take each other's hand and saunter over towards the girls.

Tracy and Dominique are sipping from fluted glasses filled with mimosas and take in the incredibly impressive décor. Shadows dance all over the room from the hundreds of candles that are lit throughout. On the walls intricate candelabras hold black, white, and crimson candles. Dominique looks around the room, feeling oddly comfortable in her surroundings; she unconsciously lifts her free hand and touches the locket that hangs around her neck. Like an electric shock, that of which she can only assume to be a memory, flashes through her mind, making her gasp and quickly let's go of it. Tracy catches her before she falls to the ground and helps steady her.

"You ok? What just happened?"

"I don't know," she looks at the half empty glass, "maybe this is stronger than I thought," she sets it down on a nearby table.

She knows she just lied, but how do you explain the craziness that keeps happening to her? These flashes. She saw a woman, but it feels like her, running up stone stairs in the castle into a huge master bedroom. It feels so real, like she is living the experience, but she's never been upstairs in the castle. This is the first time she's even stepped foot in here.

"Do you need to sit down?" Tracy asks, concerned for her well being.

Becky and Jill approach the girls; Becky puts her hand on Dominique's shoulder, "Hey, you ok?"

Dominique turns around and looks at the familiar face that she can't quite place, "Yeah, just a little light headed."

"Well, here, come with us. There's a sitting room down the hall away from the chaos. You can stay there until it passes. It's nice and quiet."

Dominique looks at Tracy who nods in affirmation, "That might not be a bad idea, babe."

"Ok, you're right. Just for a few minutes."

They follow Becky and Jill through the crowded room and down the corridor. Tracy takes in the very large and expensive paintings along the walls and the incredibly tall ceilings. She can't help but wonder what it cost to heat and cool this place. Guess it doesn't matter if you're this rich.

Becky walks up to a closed door guarded by a very buff bouncer wearing a tight black athletic t-shirt that looks like he is about to rip out of with his body builder muscles. Becky nods at the man who opens the door and lets them in. The room is comfortably decorated with lounge chairs and chaise couches. Candles are lit throughout, but a chandelier wired with modern electricity dimly adds to the lighting as well. Yards of heavy crimson tapestry hang from wrought iron curtain rods adding to the comfort of the room. The bouncer closes the door, sealing it from all the noise of the party. The only sound that can be heard is the crackling from the fire in the stone fireplace.

Becky takes Dominique by the hand and guides her over to the chaise and sets her down, "Can I get you anything? A cool wash cloth?"

"Oh, no thank you. Well, maybe some water."

Tracy sits down next to her and rubs her arm, "Could I have some, too, please?"

"Of course," Becky replies nodding at Jill, "Do you mind?"

"Not at all," Jill smiles at Dominique flirtatiously then walks towards a small bar set off to the side of the room and goes behind the counter. She pulls out two bottles of water and two goblets and starts to pour the water.

"You look so familiar," Dominique states to Becky, "do I know you from somewhere?"

"Hmmm, I don't think so. But you look familiar to me as well. It's a small town, I'm sure we must have crossed paths at some point."

"Very true," Dominique responds, not quite satisfied with the answer.

Jill brings over the goblets and hands one to each of the girls.

"Thank you," Tracy responds, taking notice of her penetrating blue eyes.

"Yeah, thank you," Dominique states, noticing the lingering look Tracy gave Jill.

"You're more than welcome," Jill sits down next to Tracy.

Tracy takes a sip of water, then gulps down half of it.

"Thirsty?" Dominique asks.

"Guess I am, more than I thought."

Dominique sips her water then sets it down on the side table next to her. She rests her head against the back of the plush couch and closes her eyes.

"So, you two must know the guys that own this place pretty well," Tracy observes.

"Yeah, you can say that. We're like family," Jill responds, sharing a smile with Becky, "We're all pretty close."

"Really? So, are they cool? I never have actually met them. I've worked indirectly with them, but never had the privilege of meeting them."

"Well, maybe tonight you can meet them. We can introduce them to you," Jill states, scooting closer to Tracy.

"That would be awesome," Tracy responds, finding herself suddenly mesmerized by Jill. She turns her body so that she is facing her more, finding herself engrossed with her.

Becky gets up from the chair she was sitting in and sits down next to Dominique's feet and puts her hand on her leg. Dominique opens her eyes and looks at Becky.

"Feeling any better?"

Dominique takes a deep breath, suddenly aware of how relaxed she was feeling, "Yeah, actually, I think I just needed to sit and close my eyes for a minute. I feel a lot better."

Becky scoots closer to her and gently touches her face, looking more closely at the porcelain fangs, "Those look very realistic; very natural on you," she tenderly slides her hand down her cheek. Dominique tenses up and slowly removes her hand, "Maybe I gave you the wrong impression here," she looks over at Tracy and sees that she is totally focused on Jill. She frowns then looks back at Becky, "Is there a bathroom close?"

"Yeah, right over here," they stand up and Dominique follows her across the room. Becky opens the door for her.

Dominique looks back over her shoulder and sees Tracy and Jill holding hands and looking into each other's eyes, very intimately. She shakes her head, not believing what she is seeing, and walks into the bathroom, closing the door behind her. She walks over to the mirror and sees that some of her hair has fallen. She starts to pin it back in place as she looks at herself in the mirror, confused. They have not exactly had the "define-the-relationship" conversation, but she thought they were exclusively dating. Maybe she was mistaken. Maybe Tracy needs more than what she can give her. Maybe it wasn't what she thought she saw. She still feels a little off kilter from the light headed memory flash she had moments ago.

She turns on the water and lets it run over her hands. She wets a washcloth that is perfectly folded lying next to the sink and rings it out. She wipes the back of her neck and sets it back down, taking one more look at herself before leaving the bathroom.

She opens the door and sees Becky and Jill sitting on either side of Tracy, kissing her and caressing her. Dominique stops in the doorway and stares, not believing what she is seeing.

"What the hell is this?"

Becky stops slowly and looks over at Dominique. Gracefully and seductively gets up and strolls over to her, taking her by her hand, "Join us."

Tracy looks over at Dominique, "Yeah, come over here, Nickie."

"Are you freakin' serious?"

"Yeah, it's wonderful," Tracy responds euphorically.

Becky tries to pull her over to the couch, but Dominique resists, "If this is what you want, more power to you, but this is not what I want. I'll see you later," she lets go of Becky's hand and walks towards the exit.

Tracy starts to stand, but Jill places her hands on her face and pulls her in for a deep, passionate kiss. Tracy melts at the touch of her soft lips against hers, forgetting about Dominique. Dominique takes a look at them; Becky sits back down. Dominique walks out the door. She pushes her way through the crowded hallway and hastily makes her way towards the front door; she has to get out of there before she screams. Right when she thinks she has found the perfect person, this happens. What the hell?

From the balcony, Shadow watches as Dominique tries to force her way out of the house. He stands up, unhappy about seeing her obviously upset. He looks over at Seth, who is entertaining some ladies wearing next to nothing, wooing them with his charm. Seth suddenly looks up at Shadow who looks in the direction of Dominique leaving the house. He nods at Shadow and walks away from the girls, heading towards the hall from where Dominique just left. Shadow walks swiftly down the stairs and heads towards Dominique who has made it to the front door and outside. She pulls her cell phone out from her corset and hits her speed dial for Jordan.

"Hey," Jordan answers, "What's going on?" she asks sleepily.
"Can you come get me?"

Suddenly more awake, "Yeah, of course, where are you?"

"At the DeFleur castle. I'll explain everything when you get here."

"Ok, I'm on my way," she hangs up the phone.

Dominique hangs up and puts her phone back in her corset. Shadow closes the door behind him and steps outside behind her. Dominique turns around and looks him in the eye, trying to hold back her tears.

"Hi, there," Shadow greets, "I saw you leave, you look upset and I don't want any of my guests to leave upset," he smiles at her, thickly, but genuinely, laying on the charm.

"Oh, well, I'm pretty sure this isn't your fault. The party was cool; I'm just having some relationship problems."

"Really?" he responds, trying to contain his excitement from seeing his daughter up close for the first time since she was a little girl.

"Yeah, I suppose I'm partly at fault, though. It's not like we ever really had the *talk* you know. I thought we were exclusive, but you know what happens when you assume," she stops herself, "I'm sorry, this is not your issue. Thank you for checking on me though," she wraps her arms around herself, trying to warm her chilling body.

He pulls of his jacket and puts it around her shoulders, "Here, this will help."

"Mmmm, thank you," the instant warmth from his body heat lingering in the jacket warms her.

"Do you need a ride?"

"Oh, no thank you. My friend is coming to pick me up."

"Ok, well, I'll wait with you, if that's ok."

Dominique looks at him, feeling oddly comfortable, and nods, "That would be nice."

* * *

Seth walks past the bouncer and throws open the door to the sitting room. Becky and Jill are all over Tracy, kissing her, caressing her. Becky looks over at him and hisses at him, her fangs fully extended.

"Get off of her!" he growls as he quickly approaches them, grabbing Jill off and tossing her to the side effortlessly.

"She's ours!" Becky responds, possessively.

"She *is* not yours! She belongs to the Princess. What are you thinking you slut!" he backhands Becky across the face, knocking her off the couch, "Never take advantage of her again! You hear me?"

"She was given to us!" Becky responds, rubbing her cheek.

"By who?"

"Sabin."

"Oh, really? Shadow will be very interested in that," he sits Tracy up, her eyes are rolling in the back of her head, "How much did you give her?"

Jill looks at Becky, scared.

"How much did you give her!" he growls, swiftly getting into Jill's face.

"Just enough, not too much. She'll wake up fine in a few hours," she answers, quickly.

He picks Tracy up in his arms like a child and carries her out of the room. He looks back at the girls and glares at them, "Never again."

Becky glares back, "You're not the master of this house."

"Don't cross me," he threatens, and then walks out the door.

* * *

Jordan pulls up in her little black SUV in front of Dominique and unlocks the door. Dominique removes the jacket from around her shoulders and hands it to Shadow.

"Thank you...I didn't get your name," she realizes.

"Shadow," he smiles at her.

"Shadow, interesting name. I'm Dominique," she holds her hand out to shake his hand – he takes her hand, "Thank you for standing out here with me."

"It was my pleasure," he opens the car door for her and closes it after she is safely in.

He waits until they leave before going back into the party. He walks in, containing his rage, and heads down the hallway. He sees Seth carrying Tracy away from the party so that people don't see her passed out.

"Seth," Shadow calls out, quickly catching up to him, "What happened?"

"Apparently your brother gave them permission to drug and seduce her. I'm going to take her to my house, sober her up and try to smooth things over. She'll be ok."

"My brother, huh? I'll take care of him. Take good care of her. I don't want a single hair on her head harmed, do you understand?"

"Of course I do. I would never…" suddenly nervous at the tenor of Shadow's voice.

"I know," he puts his hand on his shoulder and stops him mid-sentence, "I know. It's not your fault. Get going."

Seth nods and continues down the private exit out the back of the castle.

* * *

"Who was that?" Jordan asks.

"Shadow. He's a DeFleur, I'm guessing, since he called this his party," she sighs and leans back into the leather seats.

Jordan continues driving down the gravel road and onto the paved country road. Dominique reaches over and turns up the radio a little to try and rid her mind of the thoughts of Tracy kissing some other girl, well, *girls* actually.

"What happened, Nickie?"

"I don't really know. It's all so surreal. One moment I was having a drink, the next moment I'm light headed and going into a sitting room with Tracy and these other two girls who…" she stops herself and sits up, "Becky. She's the girl from my dream."

"Dream? What dream?"

"The one I had about Tracy cheating on me with another girl at the carnival. This is so freaking weird. I swear," she lifts her fingers to her temples and rubs them, "I'm going insane. I'm having these premonitions and I swear I can hear people's thoughts."

Jordan looks at her, a little worried, "Well, I hope you can't hear everyone's thoughts."

Dominique smiles at her, "Don't worry, it's not like I'm sitting here trying to read your thoughts. I'm trying to block it all out, actually. And I don't even know if they are really thoughts or my insanity," her smile fades.

"But what happened? Why aren't you going home with Tracy?"

"These girls were flirting with her. I went to the bathroom and when I came out they were making out with her on the couch and she wasn't stopping them."

"What! That is so wrong!"

"Is it? It's not like we ever said we were exclusive. I thought we were, but we never talked about it."

"Yes, that *is* messed up! Exclusive or not, she shouldn't be having a ménage in front of you, unless you wanted to jump in and make it a foursome."

Dominique looks at her with raised eyebrows.

"I'm kidding, you know that, right?" she looks over at her then back at the road.

"I know," she sighs, "I just can't believe it. I totally trusted her."

"I know, sweetie," she puts her hand on Dominique's leg, "I'm sorry."

"Will you stay with me tonight? I really don't want to be alone."

"Of course I will. I'm already dressed for a sleepover," she winks at her.

Dominique looks over and sees that she's wearing her jammies; comfortable plaid pants and a sweatshirt, "You look rather cozy."

"I am," she looks over at Dominique, "and you look rather hot! Wow, woman!" she looks her over, careful to take in every detail including how sexy her breasts look. Her corset pushes them above her neckline making them look plump.

Dominique smiles, "Thanks, but I am so ready to get out of this getup and wash off this evening."

Chapter 20

DOMINIQUE SITS ON THE ROOF OF THE THEATRE, WATCHING people walk up to the ticket booth to purchase tickets for the play. The wind starts to pick up and blows her hair back behind her. She scoots closer to the edge of the roof and lets her feet dangle over the ledge. She looks down and sees Tracy waving her arms at her.

"Stay right there! I'm coming up!"

Dominique pushes herself over the edge and falls quickly towards the concrete.

"Nickie! Nickie! Wake up," Jordan shakes Dominique's shoulder.

Dominique jerks awake from her suicide nightmare and sits up in bed.

"I am not that weak! I am not this person!"

"What are you talking about? You were having a nightmare."

"Yeah, I was dreaming that I was on top of the theatre and I committed suicide right in front of Tracy," Dominique angrily retells her dream.

"My god."

"Yeah, my god. Who the hell am I? I've been so," she balls her hands into fists and squeezes her fingers tightly into her palm, "fucking up and down. I swear, I'm bipolar," she turns and looks at Jordan, "I have not been fair to Tracy. She doesn't even know who I am. She's never seen *me*, no wonder she's letting those other chicks pick up on her."

Jordan climbs on the bed and sits in front of her, puzzled, "What do you mean? No one deserves to be cheated on, no matter what. Besides, you two have been dating for a while now. I think she knows you pretty well."

"Yeah, psycho me. She knows the girl who will let her spend the night in the same bed with me one night and makes her sleep on the couch the next. She knows visibly insecure and unpredictable Dominique. I used to be laid back, maybe a little insecure, but nothing that I would bring to the surface. I didn't feel sad one moment and completely pissed off the next. I want to crawl out of my skin! I wouldn't put up with me if I was her. Was I like that before and just didn't notice it?"

"No, you've always been fairly secure and very even keel. Not really hot and cold, but a little distant at times, but I understood why. You might be feeling all of these emotions, but they haven't been obvious to me."

"I want her in my bed with *me*, snuggled up against *me* every night. But suddenly I am afraid. Of what? I have no idea. I'm scared all the time. I'm mad, scared, sad, happy, unpredictable even to myself. I don't even know how I'm going to feel from one moment to the next."

Jordan tries to hide her hurt feelings. She wishes she was the one snuggled up against Dominique every night instead of Tracy. But, right now, it's about Dominique's needs. She scoots closer to her so that she is sitting cross legged in front of her. She takes Dominique's hands and holds them, "I don't know who you're describing, but that's not who I see. I'm not trying to belittle anything that you're saying, you feel these things, but I'm not seeing these things. Aside from now, I think this is the angriest I have ever seen you. Tracy is lucky to have you."

"I'm sorry. I'm just so, blah. Maybe my iron levels are off. I haven't been eating too well lately. When I do eat, it's like I can't get satisfied. I'm always hungry."

"Does diabetes run in your family? Or low blood sugar?"

"I don't think so, but I'm going to make a doctor's appointment next week and get some labs drawn. This just isn't normal," Dominique takes a deep breath, "I'm sorry to put you through this. This isn't your issue, and thanks again for picking me up and staying the night."

"Anytime, sweetheart," she rolls onto her knees and hugs Dominique, "Don't ever hesitate to call me when you need me."

The phone rings and Dominique reaches over to answer it, "Hello?"

"Good morning, honey. You awake yet?"

"Oh, hi, Mom. I just woke up. What's up?"

"Nothing much, just felt like I should give you a call."

"You know it freaks me out when you do that."

"Why, what happened?"

"I just woke up from a nightmare and basically just flipped out about not feeling normal for the past several months and it feels like I am feeling progressively worse," she states rapidly.

"What do you mean by worse?"

"I'm just so easily agitated these days and I'm always hungry."

"Oh," Jade responds softly.

"You say 'oh' like you know something I don't."

"Well, honey, there's something I need to talk to you about. Can you come over?"

"Jordan is here right now."

"Jordan?"

"Yeah, it's a long story."

"Ok, well, you should probably come over alone. Nothing against Jordan, but if after you hear what I have to say you want to tell her, go for it. I just don't want to say it in front of her and have you wish she didn't know."

"Ok, Mom, you're freaking me out. I'm going to shower and come over."

"Ok, I'll make some food."

"Steak sounds good, weird for breakfast, I know, but these cravings."

"I'm on it."

"Bye."

"Bye."

Dominique hangs up the phone.

"What's up?"

"I'm going to go to my mom's; she said I should come alone. Do you mind?"

"No, not at all."

"You can hang out here if you want."

"Oh, that's ok. I have laundry and stuff to do at home. I'll just see you later."

Dominique kisses Jordan on the forehead then rolls out of bed, "Thanks again, you're a true friend."

Chapter 21

DOMINIQUE, HAIR STILL WET FROM HER SHOWER, SITS AT HER mom's kitchen table while Jade sears the steak in her cast iron skillet. Dominique stirs her iced tea in the awkward silence that has filled the room; a new sensation in her mother's home. She has always felt comfortable around her mom. Now she feels like she is sitting in a strangers kitchen.

Jade plates the steak that immediately starts to pool red liquid onto the white platter. She takes the meat over to Dominique and sets it down in front of her. She sets a bowl of oatmeal at her place setting and sits down cattycorner to her daughter. She picks up her spoon and stirs her apple cinnamon flavored oatmeal while Dominique starts to devour her steak.

"Thank you, Mom. This is exactly what I was craving."

"I know," she takes a small bite of her oatmeal then sets the spoon down next to her bowl. She takes in a deep breath the exhales, "Ok, I'm going to just get to it. There's no easy way to say this, so I'm just going to say it."

"Ok," Dominique wipes her mouth.

"You're not anemic."

"I'm not?" she asks perplexed.

"No. You're part vampire."

Dominique smiles, then puts her napkin down, "Ok, Mom, whatever."

"I'm not kidding. Your father is half-vampire, which means you carry the gene, too. Your body is going through the changes that will officially make you a vampire on your twenty-sixth birthday; the age you will always appear to be once you are completely turned. The age that your father appears to be," she spits the words out as fast as she can so she gets it all out before losing the nerve to do so.

"My father is dead," relaying the facts she believed were true.

"Yes and no."

"Yes and no?"

"Technically, he is undead."

"Ok, you're not making any sense," not believing her mom, she takes another bite of her steak.

"The dreams you're having, the mood swings, the desire for blood that can't quite be satisfied, all these things are leading up to your change."

Dominique looks at the somber look on her mom's face and suddenly realizes that the seriousness in her tone, "I don't believe you. Why are you saying this? I don't want to change," she starts to become anxious and confused.

"I'm so sorry, honey."

"What do you mean, you're sorry? You're kidding, right? This is just a joke? I'm bipolar or something. Not a vampire. Vampire's don't exist."

"That's what I thought. Then I got pregnant. God, honey, I don't know how to explain all of this. It's time you met your father. He can explain this to you."

"Meet my father? My dead father?" she responds frustrated. Feelings of betrayal start to build up inside.

"I know, I know. I'm sorry."

"You're sorry? Are you feeling ok? You're not making any sense. I'm going to make an appointment with my doctor next week, then all of this will make sense."

"It won't help. You will still feel the way you are feeling, only it will get worse."

"Worse, great, Mom. You may want to seek professional help."

Dominique leans over towards her mom. Gently, she cups her moms chin and looks into her eyes, "Hmmm, it doesn't look like you're on drugs."

Jade takes her hand and holds it, "I should have told you sooner, but I didn't know how. God, Nickie, I wish there were another way. Maybe there is now. I haven't talked to your father about it in years."

Flashes of her childhood flood her mind. Her mom never implied that she could not make the house payment, she always had food on the table, clothes on her back and the clothes weren't from a second hand store and usually were some kind of name brand. Not outrageous brands, but not brands that someone struggling financially would pay for. As far back as she can remember her mom pursued painting and displaying the art in her little shop. Sales were slow to go, especially in the beginning. Reality fills her eyes as all the dots in her mind start to connect forming the financial picture.

"Is that where our money comes from? I mean, I know you have the gallery, but does it pay for all of this?"

"Your father set up an account for us when you were born and insisted that we use it. I make decent money, but a lot of what got us going, the gallery going, was your father's money."

Dominique's skin starts to pale as the blood rushes away from her brain. She puts her head in her hands to try and stop the vertigo.

"Honey, you ok?"

Dominique tries to make sense of what her mom is asking. She blinks her eyes a few times to wipe away the blur. The ringing in her ears starts to subside and she takes a deep breath.

"I've been having these dreams about vampires. Then I saw this guy, a blond creepy guy at the fair. I saw him at the costume party last night too."

"That would be Sabin, he's your uncle. He has visited me in my dreams before, too. It's one of his powers."

"He can invade my mind whenever he wants?" she asks, aggravated.

"You can block him, or any of them with that power, it just takes practice. You have powers, too."

"What are you talking about?"

"Remember when you were around five years old and we were sitting on the floor playing a game? I was looking at you and thinking how beautiful you are and you replied, 'you're beautiful too, Mommy,' remember? I knew then that you had the power to read minds. I started blocking you after that."

Dominique thinks back to that moment. Other events start streaming through her mind like a movie reel. Memories of sitting in her Kindergarten class at the round table with classmates and realizing she knew what they were thinking. When she was in junior high she would *pretend* to be psychic, or at least she thought she was pretending, and would guess with one hundred percent accuracy the object someone was holding. Her friends assumed she had someone working in cahoots with her, telling her somehow what the object was. The more accurate, the more she realized it wasn't a coincidence. She stopped doing it out of fear that she would be labeled a freak.

"I've always thought that I could hear people's thoughts, but I figured it was my imagination. But that doesn't mean I'm a vampire. I could have telepathy. He could have telepathy. I saw him during the day, the sun was out. If he was a vampire, he would have fried. I would fry."

"Yeah, that's what I thought too. You know how sensitive your skin is to the sun? More sensitive than normal. He's a half-breed. The sun doesn't kill him, but it doesn't feel great for long periods of time. Your father will be able to explain all of this better and help you with your powers and the change. There is a lot you need to learn."

Dominique leans forward and rests her chin on her hands and looks deep into her mom's eyes, looking for some sign that she is joking. She doesn't get one. All she can see is seriousness laced with fear and defeat. Dominique knows without a doubt that her mom is not making any of it up. This is real. Vampires are real and she is one.

As the reality starts to set in and fear creeps up from her gut to her heart she asks, "Do I have to change?"

Reluctantly she responds, "They said yes twenty-five years ago."

Dominique sits back in her chair and puts her hands over her face, "Where does he live?"

"The DeFleur castle."

"My father is a DeFleur and he lives in a creepy castle? Appropriate. Let me guess, his nickname is Shadow." Dominique slowly gets to her feet, Jade gets up too, "First my girlfriend cheats on me, then I find out I'm a vampire. Wonderful. I guess I better go see him."

"Yeah, Shadow. How did you know?"

"I had a rather pleasant conversation with him last night waiting for Jordan to pick me up."

"What do you mean Tracy cheated on you?"

Dominique throws her arms in the air, "Whatever. It doesn't matter right now. I've gotta go."

"I'll get my purse."

"No, Mom, I want to go by myself. I'll call you later."

Jade grabs Dominique's arm, "Hey."

Dominique turns around and sees the sad look in her eyes, "Mom, it's ok. I'll be fine. I'll figure this out. I'm not mad at you."

Jade hugs Dominique, "I love you. I never meant to cause so many problems."

"I know. I'll call you as soon as I leave."

Chapter 22

DOMINIQUE DRIVES HER CAR DOWN THE LONG GRAVEL driveway that leads up to the castle. Other cars are parked along the circle drive so she pulls up behind one and cuts the engine. She looks in the mirror and grabs a scrunchy from around her gear shift and casually pulls her hair up. Glimpsing one more time in her review mirror to check out her face and hair she decides that it's as good as it's gonna get. She gets out of her car and makes her way towards the front door and lifts the heavy wrought iron door knocker and lets it drop.

Moments later the door opens and Francesca stands there in a leather outfit.

"You look just like your grandmother," she gasps as she takes in Dominique, "I thought I was looking at her ghost last night."

"Ok, well, I'm glad everyone else knows who I am related to. I'm here to see Shadow."

"I figured. Come in."

Dominique walks into the entry way and looks around. People are still cleaning up from the party the night before. Francesca starts walking down the hall towards the study; Dominique follows.

"It's about time your mother told you who your father is. She should have told you a long time ago," Francesca arrogantly states.

"Are you related to me?"

"No, I work here."

"Yeah, well, then I don't see what business it is of yours what my mother tells me or when she tells me."

Francesca turns around and looks her in the eyes, "Be careful, little girl."

Dominique takes a step closer, invading Francesca's personal space. Fueled with anger she responds, "No, you be careful. I've just been given some crappy ass news and I'm not in the mood for some slutty maid to give me shit about my life. You don't want to fuck with me."

Francesca starts to say something when she looks past her and sees Sabin.

"You might want to listen to her, Francesca."

Dominique turns around and is greeted with the familiar face from her dreams.

"Now why don't you go and get us something to drink. Is iced tea ok?"

"Perfect."

Francesca nods and scurries off to dutifully complete her task.

He stretches out his arm and puts it around Dominique's shoulder, "Come, have a seat."

He directs her towards the plump leather couches in the study. To the side of the room she sees the chaise and thinks back to the night before when Tracy was sitting there, being seduced by Becky and Jill. She clenches her jaw, pissed off.

"Don't mind Francesca, she can be a bit jealous."

"Bitch is a better description."

Sabin laughs, "Yes, I suppose that vernacular would be appropriate," he takes in a deep breath, "You are beautiful. A good combination of your mother and father. Even more beautiful than what you think of yourself."

"What? What makes you think you know what I think about myself? she asks with her guard up.

"Well, I saw you in your dreams, though I can only see the image of you that you portray of yourself. You should not think so little of yourself."

"Yeah, well, that brings up questions on how I can block you from invading my privacy."

Sabin smiles, revealing a little fang, "Yes, well, that will take practice and power. Both of which you will have soon."

Dominique's eyes focus on his fangs, she can't seem to make herself look away.

"Oh, sorry about that," he focuses his energy on retracting his fangs; they slowly go back into place and appear to be regular canines, "I don't usually worry about them while at home."

"So they *are* real."

"Very."

"Fabulous," she sarcastically comments under her breath.

Francesca comes back in with a tray of tea and glasses and sets them down on the coffee table.

"Anything else, my lord?"

"'Tis all. You can go," he dismisses her with the flip of his hand.

Francesca nods and leaves the room.

"So, you're my uncle?"

"Yes, I am your father's twin."

Shadow walks in the room, "But not identical. I am much better looking," he smiles wide and walks over to Dominique, "I've been waiting for this moment for so long!"

"Well, I thought you were dead," she replies, dryly.

Shadow starts to touch her face, but decides to sit across from her on the facing couch.

"I guess that was the easiest way for your mom to explain the situation," his tone changes from normal to melancholy, "How is your mom?"

"She's fine, but she is not why I am here."

"Feisty," Sabin retorts.

"She must get that from you," Shadow snaps back.

"I like it," he replies full of arrogance and pride that some of his attributes have made it into his niece.

"Hello, I am still in the room," she points out annoyed.

"Sorry, go on."

"So what's the deal? I'm a freak? I'm going to want to start murdering people on my birthday? What's up and how do I get out of it?"

"Well," starts Shadow, "you're not a freak. There are thousands of us in the world. You won't necessarily want to start murdering people once you are turned, but your aggression levels will rise around the full moon. As far as how to get out of it, well, you can't. It's your birthright."

"If it's my 'birthright' that implies I have a right. I would like to execute my right to stay human."

"You were never fully human. You were born part vampire, you can't change that. It would be like being born a cat and wanting to be a dog; not possible."

"My mom said something about you having to do something to me in order for this to happen. What if I just don't do it?"

"We believe that you could go crazy and become a rogue vampire. We have to put rogue's down. They run amuck killing everyone in their paths including the ones that they once loved," Shadow replies.

"You believe it could happen, but you're not sure?" she sinks into the couch while images of killing the people she loves race through her mind.

"You are the first half-breed to be born without the mother going through the change herself. We really are not sure what will happen."

"Ok, then I won't do it. Lock me up on my birthday and we will find out."

"You would rather die than become who you are?" Sabin gasps, shocked by her statement.

"Yes."

"That is not an option!" Sabin growls, slamming his fists against the overstuffed arm rests of his chair.

"Why not?" Dominique straightens back up in her seat, ready for a fight.

Sabin takes in a breath and tries to reign his anger in, "You have been born a Princess. You will be the first Princess in our line in centuries and with that title comes responsibility and privilege. You will eventually become Queen. Have you no honor?"

She scoots up towards the edge of the couch, frustrated, "Why would I have honor when I don't even know this side of the family? Why would I want to be a blood sucking bitch that creeps people out?"

"We're not all monsters," Shadow replies.

"You mean to tell me you don't hunt humans for sport to drain them of their blood?"

"Well, not as often," Sabin replies nonchalantly.

Shadow shoots Sabin a glance, "Not all of us hunt. Some of us only take blood that is given to us willingly. Just like in human society, there are vampires who go against the laws. They are punished. We have created a system through which blood banks have been set up. People go in and donate their blood. Part of the donations go towards our survival and part of the donations go back into society and are donated to hospitals and clinics."

"Do people know when they are donating blood it is not necessarily going towards saving someone's...scratch that...a humans life?"

"Of course not. Our race would be wiped out if too many people knew that we existed," Sabin replies.

"So, these human's come into your banks, donate blood thinking they are doing a good deed for another human and get what from it?"

"Well, you've heard of a pint for a pint? We coined that phrase," Sabin replies as if a pint of ice cream should be more than enough to compensate for the blood donation.

"What?"

"Vampires make ice cream too. We're everywhere. We are totally integrated into society and play our part to look human to the outside world."

"Well, some of us have to. That's part of the privilege of being of royal blood," Sabin replies pretentiously.

"I guess snobbery is also a privilege."

"For some of us, yes," Shadow glances at Sabin, who is looking at his manicured nails.

"Look, Dominique, I am so sorry that I was not able to be a part of your life. I think if I were, this day would not be so difficult for you. You would have more of an appreciation for our culture, your culture. But if you will allow me to be a part of your life from now on, I truly believe that I can help you make the right decision."

Dominique takes a deep breath. He seems like such a fantastic man. Sabin is a bit narcissistic, but how awesome to be able to get to know her father? Maybe being a vampire, completely, would not be so bad if she can still hold on to her humanity. She is, after all, a half-breed.

"Ok. I'll make a deal with you. You teach me about my background and tell me all the good and the bad about what this decision means, and I will consider it. Otherwise, I would rather die than take a chance of turning on those that I love."

"Deal," Shadow stands up and puts out his hand.

Dominique stands up and shakes his hand. She suddenly feels calm and nostalgic, as if she has felt his hand before. She allows the handshake to turn into a hug, squeezing him in an embrace that she has been without for years.

"It is so good to be able to do this," Shadow states.

"I feel comfortable with this. It's like I've done this before," she pulls back, "is someone playing mind tricks on me right now?"

"No, this is your body remembering back to a time when I did hold you. You were very little, maybe two years old."

She quickly hugs him again and tries to remember back to being two years old, "I'm going to go. I need to be alone to think."

"Introspective, just like your father," Sabin observers.

"Definitely not like your uncle."

Dominique smiles as she pulls away from Shadow.

"Before you go, I want you to take this," Shadow walks over to the built in book case that takes up an entire wall of the room and pulls out a very old, tattered leather bound book, "Here, it's a journal written by your grandmother, for whom you are named after. She talks about her transition and life before and after the change. It might help you."

Dominique takes the book from him and rubs her hand over the design on the cover; it reminds her of the carved jewelry box her locket came in, "It's beautiful."

"It is a very important part of our history, please keep it well. I will tell you the ending when you bring it back."

"Ok."

She starts to leave the room, then turns around to look at them both.

"I'm glad I finally got to meet you. Even you, Sabin. Just, stay out of my head, ok?"

Sabin sighs dramatically, "For now."

Dominique walks out of the room and down the corridor. Sabin waits until he hears the front door close before he starts to talk.

"You know, there is no choice in the matter. She has to make the change."

"I know, but…"

"But you don't like to force people to do anything they don't want to do," he mocks.

"That's right, and especially true for my own flesh and blood."

"Our reign has been without a queen for too long, Brother. The elders are getting restless and will resort to extreme actions if she does not take the throne."

"I know, and I will work on her. I just don't want it to be traumatic for her."

"What will be traumatic for her is if the others sense her weakness and assassinate her so that wench, Matilda, can take the throne. You know they will try to force us out as well. They have been patient with us for twenty-five years. I will take measures to convince her to make the change if I have to and I will not allow you to stop me this time."

Shadow scowls at his brother, "What do you mean?"

"She has a weakness. And if that girl she is with is one of the reasons why she won't make the change, then she will have to be dealt with."

"That could backfire on you, Brother. She has feistiness and determination in her blood on both sides of the family."

"She will be convinced."

"Just let me do what I need to do. We have three months until her birthday. That gives me three months to convince her to make the change willingly. No, I did not convince Jade to make the change, but she never told a soul about us. She kept her word."

Sabin stands up, "You have three months, then things will be done my way."

"Fine."

Chapter 23

TRACY IS LYING ON A KING SIZED BED, OUT OF HER COSTUME and makeup and wearing an oversized long sleeved t-shirt and pajama pants. She rolls over on her back and opens her eyes. Panic starts to set in as she suddenly realizes she has no clue where she is. She sits up suddenly, grasping her head as the sudden movement causes a horrific headache to set in. She lies back down and rubs her head. Seth walks into the room in jeans and no shirt, with two cups of coffee.

"You're awake, good," he offers her a cup of coffee and then sits down at the end of the bed.

"Seth," she takes the mug from him and takes a sip of the creamy coffee, "How? Where?"

"This is my house. You're fine. I brought you here after those two bitches tried to seduce you."

"God, Nickie! I thought that was a dream!" she tries to get out of bed, but is stopped by the exploding pain bursting through her head.

"Ah, let me get you some aspirin and water," he walks into the master bath and comes back out with a glass of water and a couple of pills. She looks at them, making sure they are what he says they are, then takes them.

"Thank you."

"You're welcome."

She leans back against the head board and wraps her hands around the mug, taking another drink of the caffeinated taste of heaven, "They drugged me?"

"Yeah, between that and the mind games, you didn't have a chance."

"Mind games?"

"Yeah," he sits more comfortably at the foot of the bed, crossing his legs and taking a sip of his coffee, "I need to tell you something that you may have a hard time believing, but it's all true. Just hear me out."

"Ok," she responds tentatively.

"Those girls are vampires. They can persuade people through glamour, and eye contact is of key importance. You must have made eye contact with one of them."

She thinks back to Jill and her penetrating blue eyes. She looks at him unbelieving, "Vampires, right. I need to call Nickie," she unsuccessfully tries to sit up again.

"Dominique is fine. Jordan took her home and, from what I understand, she has already spoken with her father, Shadow, getting ready for her own transition."

"What are you talking about?"

"She's the princess, the next in line to take the throne. She's a DeFleur," he states matter of fact while taking another sip of his coffee, "Is your coffee ok? I wasn't sure how you took it so I made it how I like it."

"Yeah, lots of sugar and milk, excellent, thanks," she tries to process everything she has just heard, still unbelieving.

"I know, it's surreal, but it is true."

191

"Next thing you're going to tell me is that werewolves exist," she states dryly.

"I kinda like the term lycan, but to each their own," he calmly takes another sip of his coffee and crossing his leg over the other.

She shakes her head, "Where's the camera? You have got to be kidding."

"Let's just say I'm not wearing contacts. I just wear sunglasses the rest of the time so that I don't freak people out."

She looks closer at his eyes, remembering the first impression she had of him in her shop. She couldn't see any contacts, "Fantastic."

"I like it. It could be worse."

"Yeah, I'm sure it could," she sets her mug on the nightstand and leans back against the headboard, closing her eyes.

"This was easier than I thought it would be."

"What's that?"

"Telling you this. You seem ok with it all."

"Give it a sec to set in, allow my headache to go away and then I'm sure the freak out will come," she rubs her head the way she does when a migraine is coming on, "In all honesty, I'm not sure what to make of it all. I've seen too many things I can't explain. Right now I just really want to check in on Nickie and make sure she is ok. I would never purposely do anything to hurt her."

"I'll take you to your car when you're feeling up to it. You can take a bath, if you want. It might help make you feel better."

Tracy looks at him, wondering if she should really trust him. He sees the doubt in her eyes and gets up to sit next to her.

Looking her in the eye so she can see his sincerity, "You are safe here with me. I give you my word. My allegiance is to Dominique and who she loves and who she wants protected, I will protect, ok?"

Believing his words she replies, "A bath sounds like a really good idea. I really need to relax."

"I'll go start it for you," he gets up off the bed and heads towards the bathroom.

She takes a deep breath and closes her eyes again. The things she finds herself involved in really throws her sometimes. What if this is real? Who knows? What she knows is real is that she was drugged and seduced by a couple of bitches who might have ruined her relationship with the most amazing woman she has ever met or been with. She can't allow that to happen.

Chapter 24

DOMINIQUE SITS IN HER LIVING ROOM ON HER BIG COMFY couch in her jammies, wrapped in her favorite fluffy blanket with a hot cup of chamomile tea next to her on the coffee table. She sets the journal Shadow gave her on her lap and rubs her hand over the leather cover. She lifts the book to her nose and inhales deeply, gathering in the scent of leather and old paper. Setting it back on her lap, she opens up the cover and reads the inscription written on the inside cover, *The Diary of Dominique DeFleur.* Turning the page, she reads the first entry dated May 20, 1400.

> *I decided to take a walk this evening. It was such a beautiful night that I could not resist, even against the request from my oldest sister that it is not safe for a young lady to leave the house unattended at night. The air smelled fresh, the way it does after a cleansing rain, and just enough wind to raise the hair on the back of my neck. I stood in the center of town, next to the fountain, and closed my eyes, letting it all*

take over my senses when a gentleman approached me. I opened my eyes; I could feel him coming towards me, but I could not see him in my mind like I can so many others. I opened my eyes and there he was, walking with a fashionable cane and tipping his top hat. He had the purest blue eyes I have ever seen; very gentle soul.

We started talking, everything felt so comfortable and so natural that I did not hesitate when he suggested that we sit on the benches within the nearby gazebo. We talked for so long that before I even realized it, the sun was starting to come up. After consenting to another meeting this night, I rushed home. My sister was furious with me, but as excited as I am about this gentleman, Kristof DeFleur is his name. I cannot wait to see him again!

Dominique flips through the pages; interested in the story of her ancestor, but wanting to get to the meaty part, like how she became a vampire. Little things like that. She stops suddenly when she scans over the word *witch*. She quickly scans through the entry and finds that it is an exact replica of the dream that she had of being chased down the dark alley way. She rubs her hand over the page and is suddenly flashed back to the dream she had of running from the mob. Automatically, she starts flipping through the rest of the journal, rubbing her palm across the pages. Images of the memories overwhelm her mind showing her bits and pieces of a life of being human, being pregnant, and then becoming a vampire. She quickly sets the book down next to her and gasps as she is brought back to reality. Rubbing her head, she tries to figure out what the hell just happened to her. She has yet to experience touching something and obtaining the memories – aside from the locket. It was like having all of the air sucked from her lungs while piles of information was stuffed into her brain.

The muscles in her neck have tightened so hard that she feels like she has atrophied into stone. She starts rubbing her neck, trying to rub the tension out. She leans over to her coffee table to get her mug and jumps about three feet into the air when she hears someone knocking at her door.

She pops off the couch, looking over at the clock on her DVD player; ten-thirty. Kinda late for a visitor, kinda late period. She had been reading for three hours and it only felt like she was reading for a few minutes. *Where did the time go? Was I really out of it that long?*

She opens the door and sees Tracy standing there, looking distressed and hardly able to make eye contact.

"Oh, hi," Dominique states, distances herself physically and emotionally – determined to throw her walls back up to lessen the hurt she is already experiencing.

"Hey. Can I come in?"

What could it hurt?

"Sure," she stands aside, making room for Tracy to come in.

Tracy walks in; Dominique closes and locks the door behind her.

"Can I get you something to drink? Tea? Water?"

"Uh, no thank you, not right now."

"Ok," she walks past her and into the living room. She sits back down where she was reading moments ago, crossing her legs and grabbing her blanket to comfort herself.

Tracy sits down on the opposite couch and takes a deep breath, "I am so sorry over what happened."

"Hmmm, ok," she pulls the blanket tighter against her body, trying to keep her emotions to a minimum.

"Ok, I can explain it all. And, before I start, nothing happened. Seth came in and stopped them before it got out of hand."

"What do you mean he stopped them? You didn't seem to mind having them all over you," she retorts, hurt.

"They drugged my drink, and they are vampires so they used mind control, and werewolves exist," she takes a breath as she tries to explain all that she has recently learned – having a hard time believing it all. She puts her face in her hands and wipes it, trying to focus.

Dominique unwraps herself and sets her blanket aside, trying to figure out how much she should tell Tracy without sounding like a complete freak.

"I know, I know, it sounds crazy. It sounds crazy to me, too, but I know..."

Dominique gets up and sits next to Tracy, "It's ok, slow down."

Tracy looks at her, "It's not a believable story. It feels like a story. But know that I would never cheat on you."

She reflects back to all she has learned in the past few days, "I believe you," she takes Tracy's hand and kisses her fingers, "I believe you."

Tracy looks her in the eyes, "Really?"

"Yeah, let's just say I have learned a few things about myself today. A few things about my father's side of the family."

"Yeah?" Tracy starts to relax, feeling like she's out of hot water.

"Yeah. The biggest thing I learned is that I'm not anemic," she crosses her legs on the couch, turning herself so that her back is resting against the arm.

"Oh," Tracy responds, running scenarios in her head.

"Yeah. Apparently I am half vampire and on my next birthday I will have to make the change to become whole."

"Oh," Tracy sits back, trying to process everything she has learned, "And you learned this how?"

"My mom told me who my father is. She told about the vampire thing, but I also met my father – I'm related to the DeFleurs."

"Which one is your dad?"

"Shadow."

"Wow. Ok, ok, ok. Hold on a sec. This is all real? The vampire stuff, everything that Seth told me?"

"Apparently it is."

"So, in three months you will be a vampire?"

"I kinda already am. I don't know. I don't want to be a vampire. I like who I am. I want to keep living the way I am living."

"Yeah, but, this way you can keep living the way you are living, forever. Immortal," she lifts her eyebrows and looks over at Dominique, "You know, it's kinda sexy."

Dominique smiles and looks at her, "You think so, huh?"

"Well," she sits up on her knees and crawls towards Dominique who stretches her legs out so that she can sit on her lap, "who doesn't like to be nibbled on every now and then?"

Dominique smiles and puts her hands on Tracy's waist, "Oh, really?"

"Uh, huh," she smiles back and leans in to kiss her neck, "just a little," she softly bites her neck.

Dominique closes her eyes and breaths in deeply, "Uh, huh."

Chapter 25

D OMINIQUE, ON A MISSION, QUICKLY WALKS INTO THE LIBRARY
at Shadow's place. Shadow is sitting behind his desk, going through
some paper work. He stands to greet her.

"What the hell is going on with me? I pick up this journal," she
lifts her bag, where the journal safely lies away from skin contact, "I
see thousands of images of her life without reading the pages. All I
did was touch the paper. Oh, and other things…"

"Whoa, ok, hold on," he gives her a hug, "Welcome back. Have
a seat; I will answer all of your questions."

Dominique takes a deep breath and sets her bag down on the
floor near the oversized leather couch and sinks herself into it. In
front of them on the coffee table is a carafe with coffee, packets of
sugar, and creamer. She leans forward and starts to pour herself a
mug. Shadow sits next to her and starts to rub her neck;
Dominique relaxes at his touch and stops fixing her coffee, relaxing.

"Ok, well, it seems that you not only have the gift of mind reading, but of touch and with that probably sight."

"Mmmmm," she groans a little, then goes back to making her coffee. Shadow stops rubbing her neck and she leans back into the couch, "Normally I would say you are insane, but given the circumstance, I think I might be insane," she sips her coffee.

Shadow laughs, "You're not insane. Did you see your grandmother's ability to see the future?"

"I think so. I don't know all that I saw. It was all so overwhelming."

"Well, she had those abilities, she was a witch and, often, those kinds of things stay familial. So, you have witch powers that have somewhat developed and will be stronger when you take in our blood as well as easier to control. Some of us have the ability to shield what others can see, which is why your grandmother was unable to predict her own demise. She was murdered by a kiss of vampires who wanted to take the throne out of turn. But your uncle and I, along with the rest of our kiss, avenged her death. With time, you will learn how to control them and use them to your benefit. I can teach you."

"Well, it's getting worse, so the faster I learn the better. Everything I touch I see flashes of its history – as well as all of the voices in my head every time I'm around people. I just want to curl up in bed and stay there."

"We can't have that. You have a lot to do, young lady."

"Yeah, about that. What makes you two think that I am capable of taking the throne? Are you serious?"

"Of course we are serious. It will all make better sense to you when you make the change; it's a lot like an intense training, but all you have to do is drink my blood. You will be able to see all of my memories and stories throughout my life, as well as that of my father and his and so on."

"Great, more confusing flashes," she takes a sip of coffee, pulling in the full aroma of the bean, "Yum."

"Actually, it will be more complete and will all make perfect sense. You're thought process will speed up as the transition takes effect. You will not have a problem filtering through and recalling the memories as needed. The same with your abilities. They will be much easier to control after."

"So, if I don't decide to do this, I won't be able to control these – abilities, as you call them?"

"No, you might be able to control them. It will just take a lot more time to learn to control them – to focus them to your benefit. On the flip side, you might become rogue and become out of control. Think of drinking my blood as the difference between going insane and keeping your sanity."

Dominique nods, taking in what she has learned and drinks some more coffee, "So, playing devil's advocate here, say I make the change, not saying that I will. Right now I don't want to, so don't get your hopes up," she stares him in the eye.

Shadow nods, "Ok, I hear you, what's your question?"

"What happens? How do I change? Will I be able to go out in the sunlight? Will I want to kill people?" she sets her mug down and scoots closer to the edge of the couch, tension fills her as several more questions flood her mind, "Will I want to hurt my friends..."

"Whoa, there, hold on, calm down. I will answer all of your questions. Just relax a little. That's your first lesson."

"What is?"

"Learning to relax. The more you allow your emotions to take control, the less control you will have. You will have to learn to refocus yourself, or you could be a danger to others."

"Ok," she takes a breath and scoots back into the couch, "I'm listening."

"Very good. What will happen is that I will open a vein here," he draws a line across his left wrist with his index finger, "you will drink my blood then you will be consumed with memories. At first, it will seem overwhelming, but very soon after you will relax. Just lie back, and take in the memories. It's sort of like rolling with a high. Don't try to control it, let it take over."

"Ok, gotcha."

"After, you will be hungry. You will want more to drink, and we will have supplies for you."

She looks at him, wide eyed, "People?"

He smiles, "If you want, but I was thinking more like donated blood."

She takes a breath, "Oh, much better. As much better as drinking *blood* can be. I'm a little grossed out by this, so you know."

"You won't be, trust me. You will crave it and have to learn to control those cravings."

"Meaning?"

"Well, in answer to your questions about wanting to kill or hurting those you love, it is not impossible. Everyone's change is different. Some have complete control after the change; others have to be quarantined until they have the control. It's hard to tell with you, being born half vampire, you may not have the control problems. This is a first for us."

"That's not making me want to go through with this."

"On the flip side, if you don't make the change, the same thing could happen. You could go insane and start retaliating against those that you love without the ability to exercise the proper control. Coming into your own, who you are, will only strengthen you. You will feel more complete, more control, and more powerful."

"So, I'm screwed either way, great."

He reaches over and puts his hand on her knee, "I wish you wouldn't think of it that way."

She looks down at his hand and puts her hand on his; warm and comfortable, "You're so warm."

He smiles, "Yes, we are warm. Our hearts beat, blood flows through our bodies. The bitten are cold."

"Will I stay warm?"

"Yes. You will be able to lead a normal life. Yes, you can go out during the day and be in the sun, but you will still have sun sensitivity. I wouldn't try to get a tan," he smiles at her, trying to relax the conversation.

She smiles, "That won't be a huge change. Mom has kept my skin protected for years. Gallons of suntan lotion, hats, umbrellas. I'm not too concerned about a tan. I just want to be normal."

"You are normal. Think of the change as a sort of metamorphosis into a butterfly, a sort of rebirth, if you will. You will experience things in a more heightened way – hear things that the average mortal cannot, sense things, smell, feel touch unlike anything you are used to now. You will be able to live as you are. If you chose to stay in society, you will have to move around more. People will start to notice that they are aging and you are not."

"I'll always look like this?"

"Yes. That is why we do not make public appearances anymore."

"You don't want to go out?"

"No, I so desire to go out again. Walk the streets during the day, but we chose to stay in this area; therefore, we can't go out."

"Why did you stay? I mean, if you want to go out and be around people, do things, why be here in Podunk Tulare County?"

"For you. I wanted to watch you grow up, even if I had to do it from afar. I didn't want to miss a moment."

She looks at him curiously, "I don't remember seeing you."

"I've seen you and, as little as it may have been, I have been in your life. I wish it could have been more apparent, but that was not the agreement."

"I see," she sighs, overwhelmed.

"You're full."

"What?" she responds, confused.

"Sighing is a tell-tell sign that you're full. You've taken in all that you can handle for that moment."

"I've never heard that, good to know."

He smiles, "I'm happy to be able to teach you something new."

She smiles back, "Me too."

He refocuses, "There are fun benefits to being immortal as well."

"Aside from the immortal part?" she smiles at him.

"I'm glad you think of it as a benefit, not all do. Anyhow, you will be able to move at speeds faster than the human eye can detect. You will be able to fly."

"Fly? Seriously?"

"Yeah, seriously. It's still one of my favorite parts of life."

"How awesome is that? I've always dreamt about flying. What else?"

"You can stay underwater for hours at a time. We don't need to breathe as frequently as mortals. Sort of like water turtles. Come up for air, and back on your way. Makes for great hiding places when we are compromised."

"Compromised? Does that happen often, I mean, I've never heard anything but legends of vampires, never "real" accounts."

"Since we have started to use donated blood more often than trying to satisfy our hunger through mortals, we have been able to live a much quieter life. Secrecy is still of utmost importance. One day we hope to be able to mainstream, live like the rest of society, but until then, we must be careful. The secret cannot be told to anyone lest they make the change or are killed. We cannot risk being outed before it is time."

She thinks back to her conversation with Tracy the night before and quickly stuffs the thoughts away out of fear that Shadow may hear her thoughts.

"What just happened?" Shadow asks, noticing the change in her demeanor.

"What do you mean?"

"You just had a thought. It looked like it was troublesome."

"You don't know what I'm thinking?"

"No, that's Sabin's gift."

"Oh, well, I just thought of something I was supposed to get done today and was thinking it was about time I left."

"Ah, ok," he responds, unbelieving.

Dominique stands up and grabs her bag from the floor and opens it up, "Um, you can have this back," she gestures for him to pull it out of the bag.

He pulls the journal out of the bag and sets it on the coffee table, "I'll see you tomorrow then?"

She starts to head out of the room, "Um, yeah, tomorrow."

Shadow picks up the journal and puts it back in the empty space on the bookshelf.

"She wasn't here long," Sabin observes as he plops down on the couch.

"No, she said she remembered something. Did you catch any thoughts?"

"No, she is getting quite good at blocking me. She's getting stronger already."

"Hmmm. I suppose that is good, for her, not so much for us."

"Is she going to make the change?"

"I think she will. She's weighing out all the options."

"Well, Brother, I'm afraid we are running out of time."

"What do you mean?"

"I just got off the phone with Sedrick. He has informed me that Matilda is making her move to take over before Dominique's birthday. She wants to declare war against us and those who are behind us."

"What?" Shadow growls, "Three months is not much longer to wait after waiting over twenty-five years!"

"I know, but we are going to have to speed up the process. She sees Dominique's hesitancy as weakness and wants to try to invade us. She wants to start her new order of taking over the human population. You know she has an even lesser regard for humanity than I do. In her opinion, it's time for us to take our place at the top of the food chain. It's out of our hands now. You know how strong Dominique will be once she transitions. We need her strength against Matilda. She has to transition now."

Shadow glares at his brother, "You..."

"I have tried it your way for long enough, Brother," Sabin interrupts, "now we have to go with my way."

* * *

Dominique seatbelts herself into her car. Her phone starts ringing. She quickly starts her car and shifts it into first gear.

Grabbing her cell phone off the passenger seat she quickly presses the answer button, "Hello?"

"Hey, Nickie," Jordan greets.

"Hey, there, what's going on?" she turns the car down the drive way and onto the road.

"Are you driving?"

"Yeah. I'm on my way home."

"Ok, well, I was calling to ask you about rehearsal."

"Ah, yeah, about that. I'm going to need you to take over for me."

"Tonight's?"

"No, the whole thing. I can't really explain why right now, but I'm not going to be able to finish directing. You know what you're doing. You'll be fine."

"What's going on, Nickie? Are you ok?"

"I'm not sure yet. All I can say is that I'm going through some major changes and I hope I can tell you one day."

"I hope you can too," Jordan responds, hurt that her best friend can't tell her what's going on.

"Don't be hurt, sweetie. I wish I could tell you. You're my best friend and it hurts me to not be able to tell you everything right now."

Jordan hesitates wondering if she sucked at hiding the hurt in her voice, *did she just read my mind?*

Dominique, not sure how to respond to Jordan's thought, "I will explain as soon as I can. Can you take over for me?"

"Of course."

"Thank you so much. I owe you big. I'll talk to you as soon as I can."

"Ok, bye."

"Bye," she hangs up the phone and drops it back down on the seat.

The secret is too important right now. She may have already compromised Tracy, she can't compromise anyone else.

* * *

Sabin makes his way down the long stone corridor of the top floor of his castle and walks into one of the bedrooms. Moonlight is all that lights up the room where Becky and Jill are sensuously lying in the oversized bed, drinking blood from crystal glasses. They look over at the attractive vampire approaching them and make room for him on the bed.

"Hey there, handsome," Becky greets.

"How are my beautifuls' this lovely evening?"

"We are excellent, and you?" Jill responds.

"I am well, but I have a task for you."

They set their glasses down on the side tables and sit up, realizing that this was not a social call, "What do you need?" Becky asks.

"I need for you two to get Tracy and bring her here. Bleed her, but do not kill her. You understand me? Do not kill her," he emphasizes forcefully.

"Yes, Master, whatever you want. Is Dominique going to make the change?" Jill asks.

"I do not know yet, but this is a pressing matter which needs to happen immediately. We are at risk of losing our authority, and I cannot have that happen. I am forced to take extreme measures."

"Where would you like us to bring her? The dungeon?"

"No, I want her comfortable. Bring her back here to your room. Treat her well. Bleed her enough to weaken her, that is all, do you understand?"

"Of course we do."

"Good. Then get to it," he closes his eyes and concentrates, "She is at her store."

The girls get out of bed and walk over to their closet packed full of clothes and start to pick out their wardrobe for the evening. Sabin walks over to Jill and firmly takes her by the chin.

"You will not bleed her anymore than weakness, you understand?" he threatens.

"Of course, Master, I would never go against your will," she responds, trembling.

"Good, Scion," he releases her chin, "Hurry. She will be leaving soon."

Chapter 26

TRACY SITS IN THE BACK OFFICE OF HER STORE, GOING OVER the receipts for the day. Now that Halloween is over she has a lot of cleanup to do. Not her favorite part of the month, but decorating was a lot of fun. She would much rather take down the decorations than go through receipts, but taking care of business has to take priority at this moment.

She enters in her last receipt and starts up her inventory program on her computer to consolidate the purchases with what she has in stock so that she can start her reorders. She hears a hushed sound outside her office door and jerks her head towards it. She stands up and heads towards her closed office door, grabbing her handy B51 Louisville Bomber softball bat on her way out. Quietly, she opens the door, softball bat cocked and ready to strike, but does not see anything.

"Nickie? Is that you?"

She walks out of her office and turns on a few lights. She hates working so late, but with the recent events of her life, she has neglected work for too long. Tiptoeing, she heads towards the main floor.

"Hello?" she questions, hoping that maybe one of her decorations went off by itself.

"Hello," Becky responds as she steps out from behind one of the book racks.

"What the hell are you doing here?" she asks, scared and agitated. After all, she has just learned that she is a vampire.

"We are here for you," Jill responds from behind her.

"Well, I don't want you, so you can leave," she replies vehemently, careful to not look them in the eyes.

"I'm afraid that isn't up to you. We have orders."

"Orders?" she questions, her heart starting to beat so hard she's afraid it will pop out of her chest.

Becky nods at Jill, "Yes," Jill swiftly removes the bat from Tracy's hands, tossing it to the floor, and restrains her.

Tracy starts to struggle against Jill, "Let me go! What do you want from me?"

Becky saunters over to her and pulls Tracy's hair away from her neck, "Just your blood," she opens her mouth, revealing her fangs and bites into Tracy's neck, sucking her blood. Tracy's body starts to relax from the sedating venom absorbing into her blood stream. Jill releases her grip and guides her down to the floor. Becky nods at her, giving her the ok to drink from her. Jill takes her share, but remembers Sabin's warning and stops before all of her blood is sucked out.

"Ok, that's enough. Let's take her back," Becky states.

"Let's," Jill agrees.

Becky effortlessly picks up Tracy's weakened body and they head out of the store.

*   *   *

Dominique is pacing in her living room with her cell phone attached to hear ear. She has been trying to get a hold of Tracy all evening without success.

"Hi, this is Tracy. I am unavailable right now, but if you leave your name, number, and a brief message, I will be sure to get back to you."

"Shit," she states under her breath waiting for the beep so that she can leave a message, "Tracy, it's me. Please call me when you get this. Actually, I'm going to head by your store and see if you're still there. I'm worried about you, please call me back."

She hangs up the phone and heads towards her front door. Grabbing her wallet and keys on her way out.

Chapter 27

TRACY IS LYING IN BECKY AND JILL'S BED, FADING IN AND OUT of consciousness while the two vamps watch her, attentively. Sabin walks into the room and sits himself down on the bed next to Tracy. Jill and Becky stand dutifully to the side and watch him assess her condition.

Sabin places his hand on her forehead then checks her pulse, "You did well. You will be rewarded."

Jill and Becky take ease with his words of affirmation and walk closer to the bed, "Is there anything else you want us to do, my Lord?" Becky asks.

"Just keep her protected. I don't want her taken. That is up to Dominique."

"What's going on?" Tracy asks, weakly."

"Shhhhh," Sabin soothes, caressing her cheek with the back of his hand, "Everything will be taken care of soon. Just rest. You will be fine."

Tracy tries to pry her eyelids open to see who is talking to her, but can only see a blur of an image in her weakened state. She nods then falls back into unconsciousness.

"Keep her hydrated. Have Seth come in and start an IV. I want her to have fluids, but no blood. Blood won't help her at this point. She'll need to change or die, but hydration will keep her alive a little longer, until my plan is complete."

"Yes, my Lord," Becky looks at Jill who, in the blink of an eye, leaves the room to get Seth, "I will sit with her until Seth comes."

"Very good. I will be downstairs waiting for Dominique to come."

Becky bows her head as Sabin stands then kisses the top of her head. You are a good servant. Soon you will move up and become more."

Becky smiles, brightening up her face, "Thank you, Master," she responds, humbly.

Sabin disappears from the room and Becky sits down watching over Tracy, waiting for Seth and Jill to return.

* * *

Dominique rushes out of her car that is parked next to Tracy's Jeep in the back of the store lot. She runs up to the back door and gets ready to knock, but sees that it's already open. She carefully walks into the storeroom.

"Tracy?" she calls out, not really believing that there will be an answer.

She continues walking through the back towards her office when she catches a scent. She freezes and inhales deeply, taking in the alluring metallic scent of blood. Her pulse starts to intensify; she likes the smell. Shaking her head to try to find her focus, she runs over to Tracy's office and throws open the door. Her cell phone is vibrating on the desk. She picks up the phone and opens it; it shows all of her missed calls. She puts the phone back down and walks out into the main store, where the blood smell is the strongest. She sees the softball bat on the floor and, hesitantly, she bends over to pick it up, hoping to have some sort of fathomable vision that will

SARA SCOTT

lead her to where her love might be. She picks it up and before she can stand straight up she has flashes of Tracy holding the bat when she was thirteen years old standing in the batting cages. The images flash farther, almost out of control, but she slows her breathing and tries to focus on what she is looking for. The images slow down to where she can pick and chose what memory she wants to explore. She continues concentrating until she sees Becky and Jill. Dropping the bat, she runs out the back of the store.

* * *

Seth rushes into the bedroom with a red medical bag and drops it down on the bed next to Tracy.

"What the hell did you two do?" he screams, irately.

"Nothing we were not ordered to do, Seth," Becky responds, curtly.

Seth swiftly gets in Becky's face, grabbing her by the throat and pushing her up against the stone wall. His face so close to hers that she can smell what he had for dinner that evening, he lets out his inner beast with a growl in his tone, "Watch yourself, peon. Remember your place and know I out rank you."

He releases his grip and Becky, wide-eyed, falls to the floor with her head hanging down in servitude, "I'm sorry. It will not happen again."

"Does Shadow know? He will be pissed!" quickly, he unzips his bag and pulls out a bag of fluid and an IV kit.

"I don't know. I know Sabin said it was urgent for you to come," Becky gets off the floor and stands next to Jill.

The girls walk up closer to him, peering over his shoulder as he ties the elastic around the top of her arm. He extends her arm and starts to smack the inside of her elbow with the top of his hand, trying to find a vein, "I don't know if I'm going to be able to find a vein! You took too much blood!" He look over his should, "back up!" he growls at them, they jump back and get out of his way. He removes the elastic and starts to rub her cold arm, trying to get what little blood she has left to flow through her. Her arms starts to warm and he can feel the blood flowing through her veins. He

213

quickly puts the elastic back on and slides the catheter into her vein, smoothly and successfully starting the IV. He grabs the saline bag and attaches it to the bed post, setting the drip fully open to hydrate her faster.

"This is only a temporary fix. She needs blood! Now!"

"I know, but our orders are to keep her alive. That's all. The rest is up to Dominique," Jill responds, cautious of her words as to not sic Seth on herself.

Aggravated, he throws away his trash then checks the line, "The least you could do is cover her with a blanket or something! She's going to freeze to death."

Becky grabs a blanket off the foot of the bed and covers her with it, carefully lifting her arm that has the IV.

Irritated, Seth walks across the room and picks up a solid oak cushioned chair with ease. He sets it next to the bed and takes a seat.

"Would one of you be useful and get me something to drink. A soda or something?" the annoyance radiates from his body.

Not wanting to risk his wrath, Jill quickly leaves the room to get him what he wants.

Seth takes Tracy's hand and holds it, "I am so sorry, Tracy. If I had any idea why they wanted me to give you that invitation, I would never have done it. God, I'm sorry," he rubs the back of her hand with his thumb.

Jill speeds back in the room and sets a glass full of ice and a can of soda on the nightstand. He pulls a knife out of his pocket and opens the razor sharp blade. The girls creep back farther away from him. He shakes his head and grabs the can of soda, using the blade to lift the tab then sets the knife on the nightstand and drinks down half of the can. Becky and Jill look at each other, curiously.

"What? I don't want to break a nail. Men get manicures too. And not just gay men, I might add," he looks at his recently buffed nails and rubs his thumb across his fingers, feeling their smoothness, "Shifting does some damage to nails and chicks don't like nasty nails."

A loud crash fills the room, like an explosion igniting the castle. Seth jumps up as the girls run towards the door.

214

* * *

Dominique kicks in the front door to the castle, using strength that she did not know that she had, but, hell, adrenaline can do amazing things, right? She pulls the scunchy off her wrist and ties her hair up, out of her face. She forcefully walks into the foyer, trying to use some of her new found senses to her advantage. Shadow appears in front of her; shock on his face.

"What's going on?"

"Where's Tracy?"

"What do you mean? Why would I know?"

Sabin walks up beside his brother, cocky, and places his hand on Shadow's shoulder, "She is here, but you don't have much time."

Shadow looks at him, unbelieving that he would once again go against his wishes, "What did you do?"

"What had to be done," he retorts, then looking at Dominique, "The rest is up to you. You can change and then feed her your blood, or she can die."

"What? Those are my options?"

"She has been bleed to an inch of her life. There's no coming back from that through mortal methods."

Seth, Becky and Jill quickly make their way down the stairs and stand behind Shadow and Sabin. Dominique looks at Seth, staring him down.

"You knew about this?" she questions, feeling betrayed.

"I had no idea until they called me…"

"Silence, Lycan. You've done your job, now you may go," Sabin cuts him off.

"I will not leave until this is settled, blood sucker," he retorts, intent on trying to save Tracy.

Sabin ignores the retort from Seth and continues as if he had said nothing at all, "As I was saying, it is up to you. Drink. Save your girl."

Shadow turns towards Sabin, "This is not how it was supposed to be."

"Well, this is how it is, Brother. We all have waited long enough," he looks at Dominique, "Well?"

Dominique takes a breath, going through all of the crappy scenarios in her mind. She has to change now or Tracy will die. Tracy will die anyway since she has been drained of her blood and will be a bitten vampire. *I don't want her to die.*

"I know you don't, my dear," Sabin responds to her thoughts, "but, if you don't hurry, she will."

"You son of a bitch!" enraged she pulls a pocket knife from her jeans pocket, flips it open then grabs Shadow's wrist, slicing it open. She latches her mouth down hard into his wrist, drinking as hard and as fast as she can.

Shadow cringes at the sudden tearing of his skin, but then starts to rub the top of her head as she fiercely feeds. She pulls away from his wrist, her head uncontrollably throwing itself back as his blood pumps through her body. Her canines lengthen, her muscles relax, memories flood her mind, but Shadow was right. Her mind can handle the speed at which the thoughts filter through her mind. She sees him as a child, hiding in the shadows, him weeping at his mother's side when she was assassinated, she can feel his rage as he tore apart the ones who murdered her. She sees her prom date being mangled and quickly moves through that memory, not wanting to recall it. She sees the conversation between her uncle and his desire to make her change before she was ready and the reasons why. Her head falls down, hanging as she controls the memories.

She looks up at Sabin, malice in her eyes, "You could have talked to me. You didn't have to go to this extreme."

He shrugs his shoulders, showing complete disregard for his actions, "I didn't think it would help, and as it was time sensitive, I did what I felt was best for the family."

Dominique launches herself on him, knocking him on the ground clasping her hands around his throat, attempting to squeeze the life out of him. Shadow tries to pull her off of him, knowing that she cannot really hurt him by choking him, but not wanting her to become out of control. Her newborn strength is so immense that he can't get her off of him. He looks over at Seth for help. Seth comes to his aid and the two of them are able to restrain her. They pull her into the dining room and make her sit down at the table. She thrusts to pull away from their grip, but they keep her subdued.

"You must calm down. You must focus so that you can attend to Tracy," Shadow tries to reason with her.

She tries to focus on his words, but the feral part of her wants to take over, "Kill him!" she growls.

Shadow looks over at Becky and Jill, "Go get the blood! She needs to feed before she can do anything."

Becky and Jill run out of the room while Seth and Shadow continue to hold her down. Sabin walks into the room, healing quickly from the attack, and sits down opposite her at the table.

"You will be an asset. An amazingly strong Princess and eventually a Queen. I love your passion!" he declares, excited from the attack.

"I wasn't trying to please you," she growls, her teeth clenched, lips barely moving.

"You'll feel different over time," Sabin responds, sure of himself as he sits back in his seat.

Becky and Jill come back into the dining room with wine bottles full of blood and crystal glasses. They put a glass down in front of her and fill it. She breathes in the intoxicating aroma and relaxes again. Shadow nods at Seth indicating that it's ok to let her go. They both release their grip and she leans forward to pick up the glass with both hands, feeling the warmth of the liquid in the glass. She brings it to her lips and drinks it down, licking her lips when she is done.

"Give her a little more," Shadow orders.

Jill fills the glass up half way then stops.

"All the way," Dominique glares at the girl and she immediately does what she is told.

Dominique drinks down the second glass then sets it down. She looks across at Sabin who motions for one of them to fill the empty glass in front of him. Jill rushes over and does as he requested. He drinks the glass then sets it down.

"How was it?" Sabin asks, amused.

"Fantastic," she states, feeling slightly euphoric.

Sabin smiles, "How do you feel?"

Dominique tries to pay attention to her body and the new sensations she is experiencing. Suddenly nothing matters to her. She feels reborn; new. She closes her eyes so that she can focus, "Strong, light, alert," she opens her eyes and looks at him, "I can hear your thoughts," she smiles smugly.

"Hmmm, guess I'll have to start blocking you then," he smiles like a proud father.

She inhales deeply, "I can smell," she pauses and inhales deeply, "what is that stench?" she sniffs again, trying to decipher the scent.

Shadow smiles, "That would be your uncles cologne. He thinks it's sexy."

She looks at him with disgust, "You're wrong. Pick a new scent."

They all laugh at her lack of fear for her usually terrifying uncle.

He leans back and shrugs his shoulders, "Some like it."

"Right," she responds as she sinks into the chair, her body relaxing more, "I feel amazing."

"Just stay relaxed and everything will be ok," Shadow advises.

"Ok," she responds and closes her eyes. Her eyes fly wide open when she hears a moaning sound coming from upstairs, "Who's that?"

Sabin looks at the girls and they quickly run upstairs to take care of Tracy.

"What's going on? Why am I here?" she rapidly asks, confusion starting to set in.

Shadow looks at Seth who gently starts to hold her down, "You must relax. You still have time to help her."

Dominique's eyes move rapidly while she tries to remember why she came to the castle in the first place. Her mind is suddenly clouded over, distracted. She enjoys feeling better than she has ever felt, stronger than ever. *I could throw a train if I wanted.* She rubs her bicep and notices new definition in her muscle tone.

"Yes you could," Sabin responds.

She looks at him, "Stop doing that!"

"Block me then," he retorts with an attitude.

"Asshole."

He shrugs his shoulders, "I've been called worse."

She closes her eyes, trying to concentrate harder. She inhales deeply and then recognizes a familiar scent. She filters through her memory and sees Tracy; every moment they spent together, every touch, every kiss. She opens her eyes wide and tries to get out of the chair, but is still being restrained.

"Let me go! I have to save her!"

Seth looks over at Shadow, "Go ahead," he states while still holding on to her himself. He kneels down so that he can look her in the eyes, "You must show restraint or you will kill her."

She looks at him and sees the seriousness in his eyes, "Then why must I help her? Why can't one of you?"

"You want her tied to you, right? Not one of us. If she is to be eternally yours, you must finish the transformation," Sabin responds.

Glaring at him she states, "I don't want you to have anything to do with her."

Sabin responds, not truly caring if Tracy lives either way, "Then, hop to it, my dear. She's running out of time."

She looks at Shadow, "Let me go. I'll be ok."

Sensing the sincerity in her words and feeling the control exude from her body, he lets her go and she hastily runs up the stairs towards Tracy's scent. She runs through the open bedroom door and sees Tracy in her weaken state lying limply on the bed. She slows herself down and tries to calmly walk over to the bed. She sits on the bed next to her. Becky and Jill stand in the back of the room, making sure they are out of her way. She takes Tracy's hand in hers, feeling how cold she feels compared to her own warm skin. She looks at the IV feeding her body fluid then looks over at her face and sees the puncture wounds on her neck where she was bitten. She starts to reach over to touch the bite marks when Tracy opens her eyes and jerks at the sight of the woman she once loved. The eyes that once held adoration now hold something different. Tracy's unconscious reaction stirs up the predator in Dominique, causing her eyes to dilate. Tracy looks into her eyes, full of terror and weakly tries to pull her hand away from her. Dominique jumps off the bed and towards the doorway, trying to control her reaction. The predator in her makes her want to attack the love of her life.

Tracy's heart starts to race; Dominique tries to ignore the sound of her prey. She steps out the door and presses her back against the wall, bending over to put her head between her knees, trying hard to focus.

Tracy looks over at the vamps, "What the hell did you do to her?"

"She's made the change. She's one of us now and in order for you to live, she must change you," Becky responds matter of fact.

"Change me to what?" she asks, trying to hold on to every thread of strength that she has left, "a monster?"

Listening from the hallway, she hears Tracy's words. The thought of her thinking of her as a monster stabs through her heart like a knife through fresh meat. She clasps her hand over her heart and tries to contain the tears that are now streaming down her cheeks.

"It gets better; it's not always like that. She's new. She'll learn how to control herself," Jill responds.

Tracy looks over at the women who earlier that day attacked her and drained her, "You mean to tell me that she could end up like you?"

They shrug their shoulders, "What's wrong with us?" Becky asks.

"You're ruthless followers!"

Jill hisses and starts towards the bed to attack; Becky holds her back, "Get out!" she screams at her. Jill does as ordered; she turns back towards Tracy, "She's different."

"How?"

"She's a half-breed. Their transition is different, we think. So far she is doing very well."

Tracy rolls her head on the pillow so that she's looking up at the ceiling, "I'm dying," she states.

"Yes."

Dominique takes a deep breath, wipes away her tears, and walks back into the room, more slowly this time. Tracy looks over at her, trying to see in her the person she once loved. Dominique stops next to the bed and looks down at her. Shadow walks in the room and puts his hand on his daughter's shoulder, trying to comfort her.

"You must control your instincts for now and let her feed on you so that she can live," Shadow coaches her.

"Live? What will I become? Nickie, are you still in there?" she asks.

"Yes, it is still me. I still love you," she unconsciously takes in a breath, breathing in the scent of Tracy's blood. She stumbles back, away from Tracy.

She looks into Dominique's dilated eyes and is overcome with fear, "You are not the woman I fell in love with. I will not become a monster," she pulls her hand out from under the sheets, revealing Seth's pocket knife that was left on the night stand. With all her strength, she plunges it into her neck, severing her artery. What little blood she has left starts to pump out of her body.

"Seth! Get in here! You two, get her out of here!" Shadow orders, blocking Dominique from getting to Tracy.

Jill and Becky drag Dominique out of the room as Seth forces his way in over to his patient. He rips the shirt off his back and uses it to apply pressure to the wound, trying to control the bleeding.

"Well?" Shadow screams at him.

"Well, what?" he yells back, "She's severed her artery with little blood left in her body! There's nothing I can do!"

"Can we give her blood?"

"It's too late for that," he looks down at Tracy. Her eyes close and she lets out her last breath. He sits down on the bed, removing his bloodied hand from her neck.

Dominique rips away from Jill and Becky, flinging them effortlessly down the corridor and runs back into the room. She looks over at the lifeless body on the bed, controlling her urges to feed and starts to walk over to her. Shadow intercepts her before she gets to the bed.

"There's nothing you can do for her now. She made her choice."

"She made her choice! She did not choose to be taken and drained!" she rips away from him and over to the bed, pushing Seth out of the way, she lifts Tracy into her arms and holds her.

Seth gets up and starts to walk to the bed to take the body away from her, but Shadow puts his hand on his shoulder to stop him.

"Let her be. Give her the time she needs."

Shadow walks out of the room; Seth follows.

Dominique sits down on the bed, rocking Tracy's soulless body and holds her as tight as she can. She holds her breath, futilely listening for a heartbeat that is no longer there. Tears of pain and fury flow from her eyes as she tries to make sense of all that just happened. She sits and rocks a while longer, until the tears stop and she feels numbness for her loss and rage for the revenge she must have. For a few moments more, she holds Tracy then lies her gently back down on the bed. She bends over and kisses Tracy lightly on the lips and then walks out of the room, covered in her lovers blood.

*　*　*

Seth leans against the window in the library; his head hanging low with the defeat of losing a patient and new found friend. Shadow is pacing the floor while Sabin sits regally in the chaise with his little scions standing right behind him, waiting attentively for an order. Dominique walks into the room with rage filled eyes. Shadow starts to walk up to her, but she forcefully puts her hand up indicating that she is not in any kind of mood to be stopped. She walks over towards the bar.

"You..." Sabin starts to speak, but Dominique stares at him with death in her eyes threatening him to finish what he has to say.

Seeing that he will not finish his sentence, she walks behind the bar and turns on the faucet and starts to rinse the blood off her hands.

"What a waste of good blood," Jill states under her breath.

Without warning, Dominique jumps over the bar and grabs Jill by her neck and rips her head off, tossing it aside without any sign of hesitation or remorse.

"Anyone else have anything to say?"

She scans the room as they all look at each other and shake their heads "no" in solidarity.

"I don't want to hear a single thought from you, you hear me? Block me because I don't have the patience to block you right now," she warns Sabin who nods at her command.

Dominique looks down at her blood covered shirt and rips it off her body, tossing it aside as carelessly as she tossed Jill's head, then walks back behind the sink in her black bra and blue jeans to finish washing the blood off. Everyone stares at her, waiting for her next move, afraid to say anything or make a move.

"I'm hungry," she gives Becky a commanding look.

Completely terrified, Becky darts out of the room and comes back in with bottles of warm blood and hands them to her. Dominique takes the bottles and watches as Becky backs away from her, back to her place behind Sabin. Dominique puts one of the bottles on top of the bar and drinks from the other. She grabs a towel with her free hand and starts to dry herself off as she walks over towards the rest of the group. She tosses the towel on the couch and sits down next to it then takes another long swig of the blood. She licks her lips clean then sets the bottle on the coffee table.

Staring at Sabin with penetrating eyes she states, "I can understand the urgency for my transition given what I have learned from my father. You should have just asked."

"If..." Sabin starts.

"Ah, ah, ah," she wiggles her index finger at him like a parent would to a child, "My turn to speak," her tone makes him stop once again, "I will deal with you later, but it seems I might need you for my plan," the threat of death for him is apparent to everyone, "As for now, it seems that Matilda was the reason for this urgency and your overzealous thinking to take from me the one person I truly loved," she glares down at Sabin with her hate filled eyes, "Tell me where she is so I can hunt her down and kill her."